SLEEPING
WITH A
PSYCHOPATH

by A.L. Smith

Order this book online at www.trafford.com
or email orders@trafford.com

Most Trafford titles are also available at major online book retailers.

Printed in Victoria, BC, Canada.

ISBN: 978-1-4269-1779-0 (sc)

*Our mission is to efficiently provide the world's finest, most comprehensive book publishing
service, enabling every author to experience success. To find out how to publish your book, your
way, and have it available worldwide, visit us online at www.trafford.com*

Trafford rev. 11/3/2009

www.trafford.com

North America & international
toll-free: 1 888 232 4444 (USA & Canada)
phone: 250 383 6864 ♦ fax: 812 355 4082

I would like to thank my editor, Pat Kozak,
for her help and encouragement.

Part I

Chapter 1

A T THIRTY-EIGHT I was living alone for the first time in my life. I was enjoying my new freedom. It was the little things like stretching out on the couch and reading without interruption, not having to cook or clean for anyone else, having my girlfriends over for long, uncensored girl-talks. I had a great career — a career I loved — as an agent in the music industry. Life was good. I was happy and hopeful.

I had married young and went straight from living with my parents to living with my husband. It was now 1994, and I had been divorced for seven years. My two children, Chad, twenty, and Myla, eighteen, were living on their own. Chad had graduated from college with a broadcasting degree and was working as a deejay at a popular nightclub. Myla was in college studying journalism. She and a friend shared an apartment close to the college. I was proud of my kids. We got on well and saw or called one another often.

One chilly Saturday in February, a couple of friends, Diane and Faye, invited me to go out with them. Diane wanted me to see the band her cousin played in because they were looking for an agent. They were performing at a well-known country bar. I accepted the invitation then later decided to cancel. I was tired and not feeling in the mood for a crowded nightclub. I phoned Diane and told her I didn't feel like going out, after all. But when she assured me we would stay only long enough to hear the band's first set, I agreed to go.

The club was packed when we arrived. There was nowhere to sit so we gathered at the stand-up bar. We hadn't been standing there long when someone tapped my shoulder. I turned, expecting to see someone I knew. Instead I saw a stranger. He was a tall, attractive man with dark hair and dark eyes. I was a little startled — not only because he was a stranger, but because he was strikingly handsome.

"Sorry, I didn't mean to scare you," he said, smiling charmingly.

"It's okay," I said, thinking he must have mistaken me for someone else.

"My friends and I are sitting at that table over there," he said, pointing to a table a few feet away. A man and woman, snuggled close together, were at one side of the table. The rest of the table was surrounded by four empty chairs.

"We have some spare seats if you and your friends want to sit down," he offered.

I looked over at Diane and Faye. They both raised their eyebrows and nodded their heads approvingly.

We followed him to the table. He sat down next to me and quickly introduced himself and the middle-aged couple. I don't remember their names; I never saw them again after that night. His name was Joe. The three of us took turns introducing ourselves. Heads bobbed up and down as the words "nice to meet you" were exchanged.

"Sorry, what did you say your name is?" he asked me.

"Leah," I repeated.

"Leah," he said slowly, "that's a pretty name. What nationality is it?"

"English, I think."

"I'm one-quarter French and three-quarters Italian," he stated proudly.

"That's precise!" I commented. He laughed.

Just then the band started playing their own rendition of the Eagles' song, *Heartache Tonight*. I was instantly impressed with their harmonies and told Diane I thought they were good.

"I'll introduce you to them after their set," she said proudly.

I leaned back, watched the band and enjoyed the music. Joe said something to me, but the music was so loud I couldn't hear him.

"Pardon," I said, tilting my head closer to him.

He leaned in towards me. I could smell the clean scent of his hair.

"Are you a country music fan?" he asked again.

"I'm a music fan, period," I said, self importantly. "I work in the music industry, mainly in the country market.

"What do you do?" he asked, holding my eyes with his. I told him I was an agent, then returned my attention to the band.

"That sounds interesting," he said, obviously wanting to prolong the small talk.

"I like it," I replied. "How about you; what do you do for a living?"

"I work in finance; debt collection, actually."

"I've never met a debt collector before, although I have talked to a few on the phone," I said, pretending I was joking.

"Well, I've never met an agent before," he said with a smile.

We stopped talking and listened to the band. The waitress brought our drinks and he paid for the round. Everyone thanked him. I knew he did it to impress me, and I was pleased.

"That was nice of you," I said, while pushing a strand of hair back behind my ear.

"I'm a nice guy," he said playfully.

"Are you?" I asked coyly.

"Yes I am," he stated while lifting his drink as though to toast me.

"So, are you single, married, seeing anyone?" he asked boldly.

"Single," I said, suddenly very glad I was.

"Me too," he said, nodding his head up and down.

A few minutes later he gently nudged me. I gave him an enquiring look. He smiled and looked into my eyes. "Could I call you sometime; maybe take you out for a coffee?"

I hid my enthusiasm and casually gave him my business card with my work number on it. I pointed out that it was my work number.

As soon as the band finished their set, Diane took me over to meet them. After a few minutes of shop talk, I returned to the table. Joe was chatting with the couple next to him. When they finished their conversation, I told him my friends and I were leaving. He looked disappointed.

"It was nice meeting you. Thanks again for the drink," I said formally.

"It was nice meeting you too, Leah. I look forward to seeing you again."

Later that evening, I tried to watch *Saturday Night Live* on T.V., but my mind kept drifting back to Joe. I could picture his face and recall every word he had said. I wondered if he would call me. I even wondered if meeting him was fate.

When I arrived at work Monday morning, Kim, our receptionist, told me someone had called but had not left a message. For some reason, I knew it was him. I hurried into my office and started going through my notes and schedules for the week. Seconds later my intercom buzzed. Kim said Joe was on the line. I felt my face flush and my stomach flutter a little.

"Leah speaking," I said in my professional voice.

"Hello Leah. This is Joe. I met you the other night." He sounded nervous.

After the usual telephone pleasantries, he asked me if I would meet him for a drink that evening. I hesitated for a couple of seconds; I wasn't sure why because I definitely wanted to see him. "Sure," I said finally. He asked me to pick the time and the place, and I suggested a quiet little lounge that was just a couple of blocks from where I lived. I didn't tell him it was close to my apartment.

Mondays were busy at the agency and the day flew by. I rushed home after work, ate a sandwich, showered then began the task of deciding what I should wear. I changed at least three times before settling on basic black; a black long-sleeved T-shirt tucked into black jeans and a black belt with a shiny silver buckle.

I drove the two and a half blocks to the lounge. I had a bad case of first date jitters. *I don't know him. What will we talk about? What is he like? Do I look okay? Will he like me? Will I like him?*

He was standing inside the front entrance and greeted me with a natural smile. Just like the first time I met him, I was startled by his strikingly good looks.

"Hi Leah," he said, looking a little anxious. I suddenly felt at ease, a little giddy even. We found a corner table. He pulled the chair out for me and helped take my coat off. Almost instantly a conversation began to flow between us. He told me he had been divorced for three years. I told him I had been divorced for almost seven. He said he had a ten-year-old daughter from a relationship he had before he was married. I told him about Chad and Myla. He said I looked too young to have kids that old.

"I got married young and had kids young," I said comfortably.

"Do you mind me asking how old you are?"

"I'm thirty-eight. How old are you?" I replied, guessing him to be around my age.

"I'm thirty-six."

"Respect your elders," I said jokingly. He laughed.

We had fun. We laughed a lot. We talked easily and looked into each other's eyes. Time seemed to disappear. It was shortly after midnight when I told him I should go. He walked me to my car. It was beginning to snow, just lightly.

"This is it," I said, patting the hood of my bright red Festiva.

"Cute little car," he said, looking it over. I leaned back against the vehicle. He put his arms around my waist and drew me close to him. I felt warm being so close to him. He kissed me, lightly, on my cheek. I looked up at him and he kissed my mouth. It was a gentle kiss, an appropriate kiss for a first date.

"You're a beautiful woman," he said, smiling at me. He placed his hands on my hips.

You're a beautiful man.

"Can I see you again?" he asked.

"Definitely," I said with a wide smile. That smile stayed firmly on my face as I drove the two blocks home.

Later, at home, I got into bed and tried to read. I couldn't concentrate on the story so I put the book down and gave in to the relentless craving I had to think about Joe, our evening together, everything he said, his kiss. Eventually I drifted off to sleep.

I was sitting in a plush, high-backed chair in the foyer of a beautiful house; a mansion. I was wearing a white dress covered with lace. There were several people in the house. Some were standing in the foyer but most were standing in a large adjoining room. They were gathered into small groups. They all had their backs to me. I was the only person sitting down. Suddenly, my dad and my uncle entered the foyer. I watched them walk slowly toward me. I was overjoyed to see them. They were both wearing dark suits.

"My dad and uncle are here," I announced to everyone. "You can't see them because they're dead," I said as if it was a normal occurrence.

Dad was holding a long-stemmed red rose, and my uncle was holding a long-stemmed pink rose. They didn't speak. They handed me the roses, then bowed. I watched them turn and walk away. I watched them leave. I told the others, whose faces I never saw, that they had left.

I woke up abruptly. The room was dark. I felt cold and disturbed by my dream. My father had died six years ago. I had dreamt of him before, but never a strange dream like this. I wished I could ask him what it meant. I curled up under my blankets, closed my eyes and tried to return to the dream. But I couldn't. I tossed and turned for the rest of the night.

The next morning I phoned my mom in Saskatoon. I didn't tell her about the dream; I just wanted to hear her voice and know she was okay. After we talked for awhile, I phoned my best friend, Carrie, and told her about it. She asked me why it bothered me so much. "I'm not sure," I admitted. "It wasn't scary, but when I woke up I had an eerie feeling that Dad was trying to tell me something. I know it's silly, it was just a dream."

"It's pretty eerie to dream about two people who've passed away. Is the uncle your dad's brother?" she asked.

"Yes, his older brother. He died a year or so before my dad."

"Maybe he was letting you know he's with his brother," she said thoughtfully. "I know how much you miss your dad, Leah, maybe your dream was meant to comfort you."

I smiled and told her she was probably right, yet something about the dream nagged me all day. I told myself I was being overly analytical. Later that day I phoned Aunt Liz, my uncle's widow. She lived in Calgary also, but we rarely saw each other. I was surprised by how comforting it was to hear her voice. I did not mention the troubling dream.

Chapter 2

O N OUR FOURTH date, which was a little less than two weeks after we first met, Joe asked me if I had any regrets. I thought it was rather an odd question to ask so early into our relationship, but I answered honestly and said I had quite a few.

"Like what?' he inquired, folding his arms. We were at a restaurant. We had finished our meals and I was sipping on a glass of red wine. He was drinking a rum and coke and looking at me as though he thought I was about to disappoint him. I was tempted to tell him my regrets were none of his business but I didn't want to come across as rude.

"One thing I regret is not going to Europe with a few of my friends the summer before I got married," I said, as though I didn't care or actually notice the way he was looking at me.

"I have no regrets," he said smugly. He was sitting straight and looked stern.

"Good for you," I said sarcastically. "That's pretty rare, not having *any* regrets." I emphasized the word, any.

"Do you have regrets about any of the guys you've been with?" he had the nerve to ask.

"Not so far," I snapped. I could feel the anger on my face. I could feel it pulling my mouth down into a pout. I could feel myself regretting I told him I had regrets. I told myself to lighten up. "You know," I said, raising my eyebrows high, "even Frank Sinatra has a few regrets, but then again too few to mention."

He laughed loudly, too loudly, as though he was forcing himself. In return, I forced myself to smile. I looked down at my drink and watched my fingers slide up and down the stem of the wine glass. I could feel his eyes on me. They felt like a cold wind.

"I just thought you might regret getting married or something like that," he said, shrugging his shoulders to indicate it was no big deal.

"No," I said flatly, looking at him with a phony expression of boredom on my face. I turned away from his suspicious eyes and looked around the restaurant because I didn't want to look at him. From the corner of my eye, I could see him shaking his head back and forth, the way people do when they don't understand or believe something. Suddenly, I wanted to go home. I faked a yawn and told him I was tired and wanted to leave. Then I actually felt disappointed that he didn't seem to mind. He walked me to my car and gave me a quick kiss. I heard his lips smack.

When I got home I poured myself a glass of wine, sunk down on the couch and lit a cigarette. I felt oddly disturbed and somewhat baffled by his behaviour. "He's an idiot!" I said out loud as I exhaled the cigarette smoke. I watched the smoke take the words away. A few minutes later I was thinking up excuses for the way he acted. *You're overly sensitive, Leah. What's the big deal?* The phone rang. I let it ring a few times before I answered.

"Hi Leah, I just wanted to make sure you got home okay," he said softly.

"Safe and sound," I said, with an edge to my voice.

"Are you mad at me?"

"No," I lied, because I doubted myself.

"Are you mad *about* me?" he teased.

I laughed, despite myself. He laughed too.

I had flexible hours at work. A ten o'clock start time was pretty standard for agents. Our clients worked late into the evenings and were not usually available to discuss business before ten or eleven in the morning. As long as I had my schedules in place, I could take long coffee breaks and lunch breaks and leave early. I rarely did though. I was always busy and I did not want to fall behind. I felt more comfortable when I was ahead on scheduling and in my office to take calls sharp at ten. But the morning after Joe's odd behaviour, I did not leap out of bed the way I usually did when my alarm rang. Instead I lay there for a while revisiting the evening. It was the way he had looked at me that bothered me the most. The memory was like an allergic reaction; I felt itchy and uncomfortable all over. I didn't want to go into the office. It was a Friday, and I knew Carrie had the day off so I called and asked if she had time for a coffee. She did. I called the office and told Kim I would be in around noon.

Carrie was a piano teacher and worked out of her home. She always said she loved working from home. That morning, I told her I'd like to do the same thing because I was unhappy with the new direction the agency appeared to be taking. I didn't go into detail.

"It'll be at least another year before I can," I said, and then added, "I like the idea of having no one but myself to answer to." We talked about this for a while, and then I told her what Joe had said the previous evening.

"Oh, well, whippy ding for him, he doesn't have any regrets," she said while twirling her finger in the air.

I laughed and said, "No kidding!" Then I folded my arms and did an impression of him. "I have no regrets. I'm perfect. Only fools have regrets. Are your regrets about some guy?" I was amusing Carrie and myself, so on I went. "I should have said, 'I don't have any regrets about *a* guy, more like a *team* of guys. Have you ever heard of The Calgary Flames?'"

We burst into a fit of laughter that lasted long enough to make my stomach hurt. I was healed.

"So are you going to see him again?" Carrie asked, still chuckling.

"Oh sure, I think so. But I'll probably regret it." We laughed again.

"When do Ken and I get to meet him?"

"Maybe we can get together this weekend. He did make me mad last night, but, I don't know, I still like him. Actually, I'm really attracted to him," I confessed. "He's very striking and very sexy. It's all a bit crazy."

Carrie's brown, almond-shaped eyes widened in surprise. "I really want to meet him now. I'm curious."

"I want you guys to meet him," I said. "Not saying he's Mr. Right. I'm pretty sure he's not, but he is interesting and he's a lot of fun. Well, except for last night." I added something like no one's perfect, and Carrie nodded in agreement.

I left Carrie's feeling lighter; the way you do after getting something off your chest. It was almost noon when I got to work. I checked in at the reception desk for messages. I caught myself feeling pleased that he had called more than once. As soon as I got into my office I called him. He sounded relieved to hear from me and asked if I just got into work. I said I had. He was silent for a few seconds as if waiting for me to tell him where I had been. I didn't.

"So what's up?" I asked him frankly.

"Do you like seafood?"

"I love it."

"I know a great place," he bragged. "I'd love to take you there tonight, if you're free."

"That sounds fantastic," I said, suddenly feeling excited.

"I was wondering if I could pick you up at your place." After a slight pause, I told him that would be okay.

"Good. It will feel like a real date then," he said, sounding eager.

Until then I'd met him at the various places we had gone to, so he didn't know exactly where I lived. I felt strange giving him my address and I wondered why. I told myself it was because I didn't know him that well and that I had felt uncomfortable on our last date. Again, I told myself to lighten up.

As the day went on, I couldn't stop looking forward to our dinner date. I left work early and went to the mall, where I bought the first dress I tried on; a black, A-line-styled dress that buttoned all the way up the front. It was a cotton blend but it looked like silk. It was on sale, so I justified buying a lacy, black bra and matching panties. I refused to acknowledge that I had any intension of being seen in them.

I got home from my mini shopping spree and checked the time. I had two hours before he was supposed to pick me up. I put my Tina Turner tape in the stereo, turned up the volume and strutted down the hall into the bathroom. I had a quick dip in the tub; I was too hyper for a long soak. It was quite a process getting ready. I applied then re-applied my makeup. I curled then re-curled the ends of my long hair. By the time I got dressed, I was tired.

He arrived right on time, which I liked. I opened the door and there he stood looking like a soap opera star in his white cotton shirt and black dress pants, which fit him perfectly. He was holding a bouquet of flowers.

"Be still my heart," he said, patting his chest with his hand and gazing deep into my eyes. "You look beautiful." His words poured right into my heart and softened me like putty. He handed me the bouquet then followed me into the kitchen. I took a vase out of the cupboard and filled it with water. He helped me arrange the flowers, a dozen red roses.

"Thank you, Joe," I said, looking into his bright eyes. I couldn't stop smiling. He put his arms around my waist and kissed the top of my head.

I showed him around my apartment. It was a nice apartment. I was proud of it. The colours of the carpets and walls reminded me of coffee and cream; soft, warm colours that felt peaceful and safe. My favourite part of the living room was the fireplace.

"This is a nice place," he said after the brief tour.

"Thanks, I like it too, it's my little haven."

"It's nice and clean," he said approvingly. "I like that. Cleanliness is important to Italians; you could eat off my mom's floor. Her decorating, on the other hand — not so good." He smiled and shook his head. "The only thing that matches in my parents' house is the couch and chair and the fridge and stove. The rest — Oh my God!" He smacked his forehead with the palm of his hand. "More colours than you'd find in a box of crayons!"

"You're so animated this evening," I said with a laugh.

He had made a seven o'clock reservation at the restaurant. We arrived five minutes late. He apologized to the pretty, blond hostess and tipped her twenty dollars. She smiled, not *at* him, *for* him. He looked away from her and over at me. He looked at me as though I was the only person in that room who was worth looking at. Hand in hand we followed the rejected hostess to our table.

Everything about the evening was romantic. We ate delicious lobster and drank fruity, white wine. He told me I was beautiful. He told me I was gorgeous. He told me I was sexy. He said he had barely stopped thinking about me since the first night we met. I had barely stopped thinking about him, but I kept that to myself. I was high on his adulation. I felt special.

During the drive back to my place, he turned his car radio up when the song, *Brown Eyed Girl* came on. He sang along with it stretching his neck towards me when he sang, "You're myyyyy brown eyed girl." I giggled like a school girl. I felt like a school girl.

As he turned into the parking lot of my apartment building he asked if he could come in. I said yes. The minute we were inside he wrapped his arms around my waist. "I don't want to let you go," he said in a deep, husky voice. He was six feet tall. I was six inches shorter. He looked down into my eyes and I gazed up at him. I wanted to be with him.

"Come here," he said, tugging on my hand. He led me into the living room, sat down on the couch and pulled me onto his lap. We kissed the way lovers kiss. We kissed and kissed and kissed. Soon, I felt his hand slide under my dress and gently massaged my thigh. His lips moved from my mouth to my neck. His hand moved from my thigh to the buttons on my dress. He undid the buttons slowly, one by one. "God, you're beautiful," he whispered. His words caressed me. I stood up, took his hand and led him down the hall and into my bedroom.

He left early the next morning. I walked him to the door and kissed him goodbye, then raced back to bed. I burrowed under the blankets and let my mind drift back to feel everything that happened the night before; to feel his words, his touch, his warmth. It all felt perfect.

We started seeing each other almost every night. During the week we would meet after work for a drink and maybe a bite to eat. After a couple hours together he would walk me to my car and kiss me. Later, he would phone to say goodnight. It seemed like a proper way to date and get to know each other. Weekends were a different story. We went to the best restaurants, places he knew that I'd never been to before. I loved those evenings of candlelit dinners, soft music, good food and expensive wine. We talked for hours. Sometimes we went to a dance club after dinner and danced to every song. He spent the nights with me. He was a romantic, thoughtful and exciting lover. I felt as though I was on a vacation; a magical vacation.

I started buying clothes, which I couldn't afford, to fit my new life style. I was spending more and more time getting ready for our dates. He was always complimenting me. Although it felt good, it made me uncomfortable; I began feeling I had to live up to an unrealistic ideal.

One evening while we were dining he started talking about his childhood. He told me he was born in Sicily and came to Canada with his family when he was two-years-old. His voice tightened as he went on to explain that soon after they moved here, his parents sent him to live with his aunt in New York City. They left him with her for two years.

"I was four years old when I came back to live with my parents," he said. "I didn't even know them, they were strangers. I was devastated. I wanted to be with my aunt." His eyes were heavy with sadness.

"Why did they send you there in the first place?" I asked.

"I don't know. They refuse to talk about it," he said bitterly.

Joe had two younger brothers. I wondered if his parents had sent him away because they could not afford to support him. I asked him if that was a possibility.

"I doubt it, but I'm not sure. But you know what?' He leaned forward, put his elbows on the table and his thumbs under his chin. "Aunt Maria was probably the best thing that ever happened to me. She loved me, Leah, and I loved her. She passed away quite a few years ago. I think about her every day."

I smiled compassionately at him. He smiled back. Suddenly he popped into a new mood and a new position. He leaned back in his chair and looked at me like as though seeing me for the first time. "You have beautiful eyes," he said softly.

"Thanks; so do you," I said shyly.

"You have what people call bedroom eyes," he said very seriously. His expression struck me as funny. I couldn't suppress a laugh.

"What's so funny?" he asked, looking puzzled.

"I don't know, just the way you said, 'what people call,'" I said, shrugging.

We left shortly after that and went to my apartment. As we sat side by side on the couch, he talked more about his Aunt Maria. He said he remembered living in a tiny apartment, and whenever it was cold at night she would hold him in her arms to keep him warm. He said she made her living babysitting neighbourhood kids.

"I remember the day my parents came and got me. It was like being kidnapped. Aunt Maria was crying, I was crying. She kept telling me she loved me and always would," he said, with a far-away look.

"When's the last time you saw her?'

"That was the last time I saw her," he said. "My parents wouldn't discuss her with me. I didn't know how to get a hold of her. By the time I was old enough to maybe find her on my own, she had died." He sounded as though he was on the verge of tears.

"Who told you she died?" I gently asked.

He looked uneasy. "Uh, my dad. Let's not talk about it anymore. Let's talk about something else, something happy, cheerful." His whole demeanour changed from one of anguish to one of joy. The transformation was as quick as snapping your fingers. I thought he was good at hiding his pain.

"I bet you were you a cheerleader in high school," he said, sounding as though he was on to something.

"No I wasn't," I replied.

He looked at me with disbelief. "Come on, you were a cheerleader."

"No! Well, actually, when I was in junior high a few of my girlfriends and I formed our own cheerleading team," I said, suddenly recalling it. "The school didn't have an actual cheerleading team but it did have lots of pom-poms, so my friends and I made our own team. Our school colours were green and white. We all bought matching white T-shirts and green headbands. We made up a couple cheers, like, go team go, you're the best; better than all the rest!" I sang out, pretending I was waving pom-poms. "We went to every school basketball game," I said with a flourish, feeling rather proud of the story.

"So were all the jocks in love with you?" he asked, with a strange look on his face.

No," I said, shaking my head and smiling.

"I don't believe you," he said, narrowing his eyes to look suspicious.

"I know it's hard to believe, but it's true." I said, pretending I couldn't believe it myself.

"I bet they were," he muttered, more as if he was talking to himself than to me.

I looked at him closely. He was really frowning, and that made me uncomfortable. I slouched back into the couch like a child who didn't get her own way. He reached over and tickled my ribs. I giggled and tried pushing his hands away. We wrestled a little before he stopped. I told him I hated being tickled. He pulled me into his arms and stroked my hair. I relaxed and snuggled into him. My discomfort disappeared.

The following morning Carrie phoned and asked if Joe and I wanted to get together with her and Ken that evening. Joe had left just minutes before she called.

"That sounds like fun!" I said. "I'll give him a call. What do you guys want to do?"

"Ken suggested we go to The Pizza Place, but it doesn't matter to me. I just want to meet the Italian Stallion," she proclaimed.

I laughed and told her I'd call back after I talked to Joe. I called him a short time later and felt disappointed when he did not show any enthusiasm. He agreed to go but said it would be better if he met us there in case he was running late. Apparently, he had a couple of late appointments. I called Carrie and explained Joe's schedule. I didn't say anything about his attitude though. Besides, I figured he was probably tired, maybe a little nervous about meeting my friends.

After I hung up I felt so sad and tired, I decided to go back to bed. *Too many late nights.* I slipped between the sheets and closed my eyes, but I couldn't relax. I could smell his aftershave on the pillow case. The scent bothered me. I got up and put a clean pillow case on, but I could still smell it. I grabbed the pillow and threw it out of the bedroom. I slept soundly for two hours and woke up feeling restored. I stretched and moaned loudly before I climbed out of bed. The power of a nap had put a smile all over me.

Carrie and Ken picked me up. I assumed I would be getting a ride home with Joe. When we arrived at the restaurant I saw Joe's car in the parking lot. I was pleased he was already there. I spied him as soon as we walked in; he was sitting at a table with another guy. He stood up when he saw me. His grin looked slightly lopsided, almost like a sneer.

"Hi baby," he greeted, reaching for my hand.

"Hi" I replied allowing him to take my hand.

"You look nice," he said, his eyes travelling from me to Carrie to Ken.

I introduced them to one another, and then Joe introduced us to Nick, the guy sitting with him. Joe said Nick, who looked about twenty, was a client.

Carrie, Ken and I ordered pizza and beer. Joe said he and Nick had eaten earlier. He ordered drinks for himself and Nick. After we placed our orders with the waitress, there was a long awkward silence. I was racking my brain trying to think of something to say that would start a conversation. Ken graciously jumped in by asking Joe if he was from Calgary. Joe told him was born in Italy and raised in Cranbrook, British Columbia. He also said he had lived in Vancouver for a number of years before moving to Calgary. I knew he had basically been raised in Cranbrook, he told me on our first date. I wasn't surprised, under the circumstances, that he didn't mention he had also lived in New York.

"So what brought you to Calgary?" Carrie asked with a sweet smile on her pretty face.

"Vancouver just got too expensive. I wanted to buy a house and the prices here were a lot more affordable. My parents and brothers were already living here," Joe explained.

"Have you been back to Italy?" Ken inquired.

"No, but I want to. Maybe I'll take Leah with me." He winked at me then went on to say, "Leah tells me you guys have been friends for a long time." His eyes dashed back and forth between Carrie and Ken as if he wasn't sure which one of them would respond.

"No. We just met her the other day at Wal-Mart," Ken said with a straight face. Carrie and I burst out laughing. Joe looked confused.

"He's just kidding," I explained.

"Yeah, I'm just kidding. We've been friends with Leah for years," Ken said proudly.

"I met Ken about ten years ago," I informed Joe. "Remember I told you he also works in the music industry. He's a sound technician."

"Yeah, I remember," Joe said nodding.

Carrie and I began chatting about a movie we had watched on television a few nights before. Nick had also seen the movie and was offering his opinions on it. We were sitting at a round table. Joe was on one side of me, Nick was on the other and Carrie was sitting between Nick and Ken. Nick was leaning so close to Carrie she had to sit on a slant to create a little space between them. Suddenly Joe said he had to give Nick a ride home. Nick looked surprised but didn't protest. We had been there for less than an hour; we hadn't even finished eating. I felt let down and embarrassed.

"Really?" I questioned him.

"Sorry, but I've got to get this guy home." He leaned over to me and whispered that he would call me later.

Carrie, Ken and I stayed for a while and then went to my apartment for coffee. Once we were settled I mentioned I thought Joe had acted weird. "He's usually much friendlier," I said in his defence. "Maybe he was nervous meeting you."

"Weird? The guy's a goof!" Ken said in a matter of fact way.

"Ken!" Carrie said in a scolding manner.

"No one can accuse you of beating around the bush, Ken," I chuckled. "He did leave pretty abruptly." I assumed that's what Ken thought was goofy.

"I didn't care that he left. I think his buddy needed to go home, he looked pretty wasted. It was just, I don't know, something about him rubbed me the wrong way," Ken stated with no other intension but to be honest about his feelings.

"Jeez, Ken, you spent an hour with the guy. Give him chance; maybe you rubbed him the wrong way too," Carrie pointed out.

"You guys should not be rubbing each other at all!" I said, making them laugh. Just then the phone rang. It was Joe. I told him I was having coffee with Carrie and Ken and I'd call him back. The three of us ended up involved in a long conversation about music, the industry and some of the people in the industry. I forgot all about calling back. It was late when Carrie and Ken left, so I went straight to bed.

Carrie phoned me the next morning. She was worried I might be upset about what Ken said about Joe. I told her not to worry; I wasn't at all upset. "He was kind of a goof last night," I said.

"Well, he sure is a good looking goof!" Carrie replied cheerfully.

"I know," I said with a little giggle. "He is definitely good looking. It's just that he agreed to our plans last night then he brings his supposed client along. What the hell was that all about?" I vented on and on, eventually spilling out that sometimes I thought he was hiding something.

"Like what?" She asked her voice suddenly full of concern.

"Well, I've never been to his house. He's been here lots of times, but he's never invited me to his home.

"Geez, Leah. Why do you think he hasn't had you over to his place? Does he live alone?"

"Not really. He lives at his parent's house. They live upstairs, he lives down stairs," I said feeling a little embarrassed I was dating a grown man who was living with his parents.

"Are you serious? How old is he?" She demanded.

"He's thirty-six. He told me he's living with his parents temporarily because he just sold his house. He made quite a bit of money off it, which he put into some short term investments; stocks, mutual funds and stuff. I don't know, he sounds like he knows what he's talking about. He says as soon as his investments pay off, he'll buy another house. He didn't want to get tied into a rental lease."

"It makes sense," Carrie said, sounding satisfied.

"I know it does. I guess I have some doubts about him right now. It's crazy; I've never met anyone like him. He's exciting and romantic. Most of the time I love being with him, but sometimes he really, really, really bugs me."

"What's bugs you about him?"

"For one thing, he wears an undershirt all the time. Even when we're in bed! He never takes the darned thing off."

"What kind of undershirt?" she asked. I could picture her crinkling up her nose.

"Like the kind Marlon Brando wore in *A Streetcar Named Desire*" I explained.

"Stella!" we both yelled at the same time, dissolving into a fit of giggles. Once we calmed down, Carrie suggested he might be hiding a tattoo, maybe a tattoo of his ex-wife's or an ex-girlfriend's name.

"Maybe he has a tattoo that says Mommy or Mama!" I said mockingly, which led to more giggling and speculation.

I felt better after talking to Carrie. We considered ourselves to be soul sisters because we had such a powerful bond. We knew how to lift each other up. We had lots in common, even physically; we were the same size and both had long, blond hair and brown eyes. She and I had both married young; both divorced young. Ken was her second husband. We had lived the experience of divorce and single parenting. We could talk every day for hours. Ken couldn't believe we never ran out of things to talk about. It felt natural and necessary for us to be friends.

Only minutes after I finished talking to Carrie, Joe phoned. He apologized for leaving so early the night before. He said Nick was embarrassing him because he was hitting on Carrie. He asked me if Ken was upset with Nick. *No but he thinks you're a goof.*

"No, he wasn't upset. I don't think he thought Nick was hitting on Carrie. I didn't, and I'm pretty sure Carrie didn't," I said, thinking he was imagining things.

"Are you serious?" he practically shouted. "It was pretty obvious. On the way home he said he'd like to, well, I won't repeat exactly what he said, but basically he said he'd like to be with Carrie."

By the time I hung up, I was convinced his odd behaviour was because of Nick. I felt guilty for slamming him earlier. I phoned Carrie back and told her what he'd said. She laughed and said Nick could dream on.

A few days later, Joe took me to his parents' house. I was pleased I was finally going to meet them. It was early evening. His parents were both sitting at the kitchen table, drinking tea. They seemed surprised by our visit and I could tell when he introduced me they had no idea who I was. I felt bad that he hadn't told them about me. His mom offered us tea. Joe turned it down. He explained we weren't staying. I was relieved. The three of them conversed in Italian for a few minutes then he led me downstairs. Half the basement was filled with furniture; some pieces were covered with blankets. He explained the furniture was his then proudly introduced me to each item.

"This is my Italian leather couch and chair," he said, "Feel how soft it is." I obediently stroked the cream coloured leather and told him it was nice. Next he presented three glass-top cocktail tables and a formal dining room set. He also showed me an imposing black bedroom suite. I thought it looked evil, like something I'd seen in a horror movie, but I kept that to myself. Finally he showed me a box holding four different-sized, brass ornaments that looked like urns meant to hold ashes after a cremation. I stopped myself from cringing as he held each one up for approval.

After the brief visit we headed back to my place. As he drove, he did an impersonation of his parents having a conversation about us. "Why he no date Italian girl? He break-a my heart," he said, talking in a high pitched voice representing his mom. "Forget about it, he like-a the blond girl, Mama," he said, this time in a deep voice mimicking his dad. He was waving one hand in the air while he talked. His little production made me laugh, despite my disappointment about the visit.

Once we got to my apartment we — actually he — decided to order Chinese food. While we were eating, the song *Unchained Melody* came on the radio. "Oh, I haven't heard this song for a long time," I said, "I love it." I set my plate down, jetted over to the radio and turned the volume up. Suddenly, he was right behind me. He turned me towards him and pulled me into his arms, then held me closely against him as we moved back and forth in time with the music. I felt his broad shoulders and I thought they were perfect to rest my head against. He leaned his head back so he could look at me then sang along with the song. "I neeeed your love," he screeched. I didn't care that he sang off key. In fact, I thought it was charming that he didn't care either. He whispered in my ear, "This is our song." I almost told him it was about a guy in prison, but I didn't want to ruin the moment. I felt wild and passionate dancing in his arms. When the song ended he lifted me up and carried me to the bedroom.

An hour or so later we returned to the kitchen and micro waved our food. I was wearing my pink terry robe. Joe was wearing army green boxers — and the ever-present undershirt.

Chapter 3

I T WAS A courtship that read like a Hollywood script. Joe's constant and creative compliments fed my ego and anesthetised my brain. Each day after work, I rushed home to get ready for our date. It was fun to have a date every evening. Once I was satisfied with the way I looked, I sat in the living room and waited for the intercom to buzz. I let him in the main the door then practically counted the seconds it took him to climb the stairs to my apartment. He always made a memorable entrance. Sometimes he gasped at the sight of me and put his hand over his heart. Sometimes he wrapped his arms around my waist, lifted me up and swung me around while declaring I was the most gorgeous woman he had ever seen. Sometimes he just stood looking into my eyes, telling me I looked amazing. I knew this wasn't the way everyone saw me, but he made me believe it was the way I appeared to him. I felt lucky, but the pressure to live up to his vision of me was building.

Sometime around the middle of April, Joe took me to a very upscale Italian restaurant. After ordering, he said something to our waiter in Italian. A few minutes later a distinguished-looking man came over to us. He welcomed Joe with a smile and a hearty hand shake.

"This is my girlfriend, Leah," Joe said raising both hands towards me as though he was presenting me rather than introducing me. "Leah, this is Bruno Rossi, the proud owner of this place." Bruno Rossi bowed his head and gently shook my hand.

"*Bella ragazza,*" he said to Joe as he released my hand.

"*Sei,*" Joe replied with a beaming smile. "Grazie, Bruno."

As soon as Bruno left, Joe leaned over to me and said, "He said you're beautiful, a beautiful girl." His eyes shone with pride. I felt myself blush.

After dinner we sat talking and sipping wine. Joe was comparing a picture hanging in the entrance of the restaurant to a picture his mom had of the village she grew up in. Suddenly and impulsively, I slid my shoe off, stretched my leg out underneath the table and rubbed my foot up and down the inside of his calf. Even though my gesture was well hidden under the white linen table cloth, I felt a little naughty. I had never dared to do anything like that before. He reached across the table, took hold of my hand and lifted it to his lips. He looked at me longingly as he planted tender kisses on my fingers.

"May I take you home, *bella ragazza*?" he asked playfully.

"*Sei,*" I replied, in the same tone.

That night while we were snuggled up next to each other on the couch, he told me he loved me. He looked deep into my eyes, smiled warmly, and fearlessly said, "I love you, Leah. I love you with all my heart." I felt joy; pure, deep joy. My eyes filled with tears and I silently thanked God for this love. "I love you too, Joe." I whispered. He wrapped his arms around me and held me close. We sat like that for a few silent minutes then he said, "I'm going to be so good to you, sweetheart. I'll never do anything to hurt you."

For days after his declaration of love I was in state of bliss. He loved me and I loved him. He was exhilarating, exciting and passionate. I felt loved and appreciated in a way I had never experienced before. I just wanted to feel it and enjoy it. Whatever doubts I'd had about him earlier in our relationship seemed small and insignificant. He gave me an incredible gold bracelet one day and a matching necklace a few days later.

"I love spoiling you, sweet pea," he said as he fastened the necklace on me. I had mixed feeling about his generosity; it felt wonderful and uncomfortable at the same time. I tried to explain that to him, but he didn't understand.

"I want to do special things for you because I love you. If it makes you feel any better, let's say you have to give it back if you break up with me. Okay?" he said in a surprisingly matter of fact way.

"Yeah, I feel better," I responded, although I was a little confused by his suggestion.

"Are you going to break up with me?" he asked with a childlike expression on his face that made me chuckle.

"Not if I have to give you the jewellery back!" I teased.

"Don't even joke about that," he warned in a deadly serious tone.

"Relax," I said, giving him a quick kiss on the cheek. He didn't respond. Instead, he sat quietly for a few minutes. Then, as if a spell had been lifted, he stood up and announced he was hungry. He suggested we go shopping because he wanted to cook me dinner. So off we went to the grocery store. He picked up several ingredients for a steak dinner. On our way to the cashier he gave me a quirky grin and asked if I wanted to pay. I smiled and told him I did.

A few days later, he showed up at my apartment unannounced. He was carrying a bag full of groceries and a bottle of wine. I had just walked in the door, tired from a gruelling day at work and wanting to have a bath and a nap. I was annoyed he showed up without any regard or consideration to what I may have wanted.

"Surprise!" he shouted when I opened the door.

"I am surprised, actually," I said with a sigh.

"What's wrong? You look upset," he commented as he brushed by me and made his way into the kitchen.

"I'm tired. I wasn't expecting you."

"That's why I'm here, to take care of you. Now go have a long, hot bath and relax. I'm going to make you a fantastic dinner. I'll even go home early so you can get a good night's sleep."

Even though I wasn't completely mollified, I smiled. By the time I finished bathing, tantalizing aromas were coming from the kitchen. As promised, the dinner was fantastic. And, as promised, he left early. He had redeemed himself.

Chapter 4

THE BANDS I represented were Canadian road bands. They travelled across western Canada playing different venues, mainly night clubs. I also booked bands from the United States for six-week tours. As an agent, one of my responsibilities was to see these bands perform. Agents call this going on "rounds." Sometimes this meant travelling to other cities, but usually I could see them at a venue in Calgary. Occasionally one of the other agents I worked with would join me on rounds, Once in awhile, Carrie would join me, which turned "doing rounds" into "having fun doing rounds." I didn't like going on rounds alone, but sometimes I had no choice. Once I started dating Joe I didn't have to worry about that. He was always willing to come along with me. He seemed to enjoy listening to the music and meeting the guys in the bands.

Terry Douglas was the leader of the most popular band I represented. We had worked together for six years. He was my favourite client and a dear friend. All the girls in our office had a crush on him. He was a good looking guy with a magnetic personality. He had this ability to make everyone around him feel good. After several weeks on the road, his band was in Calgary to perform at one of the most popular nightclubs in the city for the next two weeks. He came to my office to see me and we ended up going out for lunch. We discussed business and then got into a hearty discussion about the politics of the music industry. I didn't get back to the office until the middle of the afternoon. I had several phone messages waiting for me. Two were from Joe. They both said: please phone me the minute you get in. I crumbled them in my hand and threw them in the garbage. I was fuming that he called twice. I returned my business calls, which took almost an hour. Then, feeling much calmer, I phoned Joe.

"I was just going to phone you," he greeted. "I left a message for you to call me hours ago. Did you get it?" His voice was tense.

"Yes I did get your messages — both of them. I've been swamped here. What's up?" I said impatiently.

"I just wondered if you wanted to meet me after work for dinner," he replied defensively.

"Okay," I said, softening my tone a little, "but I'm not sure what time I'll be finished here. I'll phone you back in an hour or so to set up a time. Where do you want to meet?"

"I don't know, I'm kind of craving Vietnamese food, but it's up to you." He sounded calmer. I told him his choice of restaurant would be fine then hung up and sat with my thoughts. I was troubled by his attitude of entitlement and planned to discuss it with him during dinner.

We met at the restaurant as planned. He was already sitting at a booth and waved enthusiastically when he saw me. I acknowledged him with a smile.

"You look nice. Your hair is so shiny," he said as soon as I sat down. He looked at me lovingly; it felt nice to be looked at like that. He reached across the table and lightly stroked my hand. I looked at him, his warm dark eyes, his beautiful smile; I was glad I was with him.

We had finished our meal and were enjoying a cup of coffee when I broached the subject of his calls. "Joe when you call me at work and leave a message, I'll call you back as soon as I can. You don't have to call again, I won't forget about you," I said smiling kindly.

"You could call me twenty times a day and I wouldn't mind. In fact I'd love it!" he replied with a sarcastic edge to his voice.

"Or you might think that I didn't respect your privacy," I challenged, hoping I was making a point.

"I'd think that you must be madly in love with me," he shot back with an impish grin.

"Maybe you'd think I was checking up on you."

"You can check up on me anytime, baby."

"I wouldn't do that Joe. It's creepy," I said flatly, indicating that the subject was closed.

He looked slightly alarmed then laughed. "I'm just kidding!"

We left the restaurant and went back to my apartment. Despite our edgy discussion, we cuddled up together on the couch and started watching David Letterman. Before Letterman finished his monologue, Joe turned the volume way down and asked me if he could talk to me about something. "Sure," I said, shifting to face him.

"I don't think you realize how attractive you are," he said as though he was telling me I had a serious illness. Fighting back an urge to laugh, I asked him what he was talking about.

"I'm serious," he insisted. "You're a beautiful and sensuous woman, Leah. All men see that when they look at you."

"Beauty is in the eyes of the beholder, Joe," I said. "I mean, I'm flattered that you see me that way, but that doesn't mean everyone does."

"Trust me; I see the way guys look at you. I don't blame them, but sometimes it drives me crazy."

"*You're* kind of crazy," I said feeling slightly giddy over his observation.

"Crazy about you!" he said, pulling me into his arms.

Later that week we went to see Terry's band. The minute Terry saw us he rushed over and greeted me with a big, friendly hug. I felt Joe's disapproval immediately but didn't let it stop me from hugging Terry back. When I introduced him to Joe, he reached out to shake hands. Joe acted as though he had not seen the gesture and simply nodded curtly. Terry dropped his hand. I felt embarrassed.

"Come over and say hi to the guys," Terry said looking only at me.

"Sure," I said. I asked Joe if he wanted to come. He didn't. I ignored his pout and followed Terry to the side of the stage where the rest of the band members were gathered. After a brief conversation the guys went on stage and I made my way back to Joe. He was sitting at the bar staring into his drink.

"Come here often?" I said jokingly as I lifted myself onto the bar stool next to him.

"You obviously do," he snapped back.

I knew he was sulking because of Terry, but I didn't care. I figured he'd get over it. I focused on watching the band. They sounded great, and they looked great. I felt proud to be their agent, but I didn't feel very proud of Joe. The band was maybe half way through their set when he said he wanted to go home. I felt like telling him to go ahead, good riddance. But I didn't. I decided I'd rather just go home and come back another evening without him. *Carrie will come with me.*

Out in the parking lot, on our way to his car, he walked quickly, several steps ahead of me. I tried to catch up to him but he just walked faster, so then I walked deliberately slowly. I didn't like the image I saw; the man walking several steps ahead of the woman. I decided I was going to let him have it as soon as we were in the car. Yes, he was going to get an earful from me. As it turned out, I didn't get the chance.

I barely had my seatbelt done up when he revved the engine and sped out of the parking lot. I felt my body tense. I shouted his name, but before I could say another word he started yelling at the top of his lungs. It was shocking and frightening. His face was dark and rigid. His eyes were glassy and cruel. He looked like someone else, someone I had never met before. I shivered as chills ran up and down my spine.

"I thought you were professional but you're not. You acted like a fucking slut, you can't be trusted!" He was screaming like a lunatic. His words flew like weapons with a force that knocked me off balance. I couldn't think straight. It didn't seem real. "You were flirting with that fucking asshole Terry, right in front me, like I'm a piece of garbage."

You are a piece of garbage. "I wasn't flirting with Terry and I am not a slut," I shouted, fighting back tears.

"You acted like a slut so you must be a slut!" he bellowed while pounding his fist on the steering wheel.

I was stunned by his outburst; it frightened me. I couldn't wait to get out of the car. He slammed his brakes on in front of my building. I leapt out of the car as though it was on fire. I hardly had time to slam the door shut before he squealed away.

My mind was flooded with confusion as I made my way up the stairs to my apartment. I was seething with anger, but I was also hurt. The whole thing seemed unbelievable. I was shaking as I unlocked my door. Once inside, I noticed the bouquet of roses sitting on the dining room table.

He had given them to me the day before and they were already wilting. *Maybe it's a sign.* I grabbed them and threw them in the garbage.

I tried to relax, but I couldn't, so I had a hot bath and went straight to bed. As I lay staring into the darkness, I reviewed the entire catastrophic evening. The whole thing seemed so farfetched that I actually questioned myself. Was it as bad as I thought? Was my mind exaggerating? Was it my fault? Maybe I *was* flirting with Terry. Maybe I *did* hurt Joe's feelings. But he was awful. He's crazy if he thinks I'm the type who would put up with such crap.

Oh God I'll miss him!

I jumped when the phone rang. I reached over and grabbed it.

"Did I wake you up?"

"What do you want?" I snapped.

"I'm sorry, Leah," he moaned as if he was in excruciating pain.

"I don't think sorry is good enough, Joe."

"You're right. I don't know what else to say though. I feel terrible for the way I acted. I wish I could take it back."

I could tell he was on the verge of crying but I didn't care. "You called me a slut!" I yelled. I was so full of anger I could have easily thrown my own tantrum. "You're insane if you think I'll put up with that."

"I know, I know and I was wrong. I was jealous and scared, I guess. I'm so afraid of losing you, I'm driving myself nuts. I'm so sorry baby. Please, I beg you, don't break up with me. I swear I'll make this up to you. I love you so much. I'm so sorry. God, I'm so embarrassed for acting that way. It's not me, Leah, you know that." He really did sound scared and desperate. I began to feel sorry for him.

"Calm down, Joe," I said mildly. "I'm too tired to talk. I'm going back to bed."

"I'm not going to be able to sleep," he whined.

"That's not my problem, is it?"

"No, it's not your problem, you're right. But please, Leah, let me take you out for dinner tomorrow night. We can talk things over."

"Okay, dinner tomorrow," I said, just to get rid of him.

"I love you," he whispered.

"Goodnight Joe."

I hardly slept that night. My intuition, which I had not learned to completely trust, was trying to tell me something; something I did not want to face. When I woke up from my restless sleep, I felt sick. I called the office and told Kim I had a pounding headache and wouldn't be in until after lunch. I instructed her to say I was in a meeting if anyone called. The second I hung up the phone, it rang. I didn't answer. I knew it was Joe. He left a message for me to call him. "You're probably in the shower. Give me a call before you head out to work. Love you."

The whole time I was in the shower I thought I could hear the phone ringing. I couldn't stand the thought of talking to him at that point. I told myself I was going to break up with him; I was fed up with his jealousy and his temper. I couldn't be with someone like him, and he obviously couldn't be with someone like me. I wanted a boyfriend, not a boss. It made me furious that he thought he could treat me like that. I wanted to scream. However, even before I got out of the shower my anger had turned into deep sadness. I knew I would miss him terribly. I had been swept off my feet, and when you're swept off your feet, you've lost your balance. I felt emotionally exhausted. I towelled myself off slowly, put my nightgown back on, dried my hair and crawled back into bed. I was sleeping within minutes.

When I woke up I checked the clock and was surprised I had slept for two hours; it was eleven o'clock. I got up quickly then took my time getting ready for work. I was grateful for the sleep and for some time to myself. I tried not to think about Joe, but he kept popping into my mind — not the Joe of the night before, but the sweet, charming Joe of the night before that, and the night before that. I tried to fill my head with other thoughts.

I arrived at work just before one. Terry was waiting in the lobby for me. We had a scheduled meeting for one o'clock, which I almost forgot about. I felt uncomfortable and instantly apologized for not sticking around longer the night before. I told him we left because Joe wasn't feeling well. I figured that wasn't a total lie.

"No problem, but I did miss you," he teased, "I wanted to do a tequila shot with you."

"Next time," I said, relaxing in his company.

On the way to my office we stopped at Kim's desk so I could check for messages. She handed me a stack of them. I quickly looked through them; three were from Joe. I felt a jolt of anger. *He should be too embarrassed to be phoning me.*

It took close to forty-five minutes to schedule a tentative road tour for Terry's band. Just as we were wrapping things up he asked me how long I'd been dating Joe.

"Not that long," I said avoiding his hazel eyes.

"He seems pretty intense."

"Sometimes," I said, smiling and shrugging to indicate it was no big deal. But I knew in my heart it was a big deal, something I should not shrug off.

I walked Terry to the main door. We hugged and said goodbye. I had an odd feeling while hugging him, a feeling Joe's disapproval was lurking somewhere. I went back to my office, closed the door and phoned him. He sounded overjoyed and told me he had made reservations for dinner and would pick me up at six-thirty. He babbled on, saying he had a lot to tell me. I didn't even try to show any enthusiasm. I still thought I was going to break up with him and wondered if I should do it during dinner or after. I decided it would be proper if I paid for dinner, or at least for my own meal. I knew I shouldn't even be seeing him. I told myself I wanted to hear what he had to say, but I began to admit to myself that deep down I wanted him to convince me not to break up with him. I was shocked to realize how hooked I was on his attentiveness and romantic gestures, on the way he could make me feel so cherished. I didn't want to let that part go.

He arrived twenty minutes early. He was wearing jeans, a white T-shirt and a grey tweed sports jacket. He looked handsome, spotless and innocent. He gently urged me into his arms and held me like he never wanted to let me go. I thought I should push him away but I was injured and his arms felt healing and, ironically, safe.

"I love you so much sweet pea," he purred into my ear. "I'm so sorry. I wish I could make last night disappear. I feel so bad, so stupid."

I stiffened and pulled back. "I feel stupid too," I spat out.

"Why? You didn't do anything," he assured me, looking incredibility puzzled.

"I feel stupid that I'm even talking to you after the way you acted last night, the things you said. You acted crazy, Joe, like a complete nut case." I felt a lump in my throat and tears in my eyes.

"You're right, I did act crazy. But honest to God, Leah, it will never happen again. I probably don't deserve a second chance but I'm asking for one. I know that you know how much I love you. Please, don't let one night ruin what we have."

"It's not me ruining what we have. It's you."

He nodded in agreement and sighed. His eyes pleaded with mine while he spoke. "Leah I'm begging you to give me another chance, I'll make it up to you, I promise." I can't tell you with words how sorry I am for last night, how ashamed I am. Let me show you how sorry I am; let me show you it will never happen again. I love you and I want to make you happy. I'll never hurt you again. Please baby."

He looked and sounded so genuinely sorry, sad and frightened that the last shreds of my resolve fell away. I opened my arms and my heart to him. He rubbed his hand up and down my back and gently kissed my forehead. "Thank you, you won't regret it," he said softly.

It was like magic the way he was able to make the incident disappear with a simple confession of love and vulnerability. We didn't make it to the restaurant that night. He lifted me up and carried me over to the couch then knelt down beside me and slowly caressed my body. He unbuttoned my blouse and undid my bra. He kissed me long and passionately on my mouth, my neck, my breasts. I felt his hand slide down and undo my pants. Soon I was quivering in a state of ecstasy. It felt like love.

"I never knew I could love anyone this much," he whispered.

"I feel the same way," I said, oblivious to anything but the moment.

The next morning we went out for brunch. He was fuelled with energy and high on happiness. We were giddy in the restaurant, throwing one liners back and forth.

"What's a nice girl like you doing with a guy like me?" he asked speaking with an Italian accent.

"Doing undercover work," I said.

He looked baffled for a few seconds then caught on. "You're good at your job, baby."

"You'd think I'd get tired of hearing that, but I don't," I joked.

That's how things went for the next couple of weeks; fun, relaxing and romantic. I felt secure and was certain I had made the right choice staying with him. I was wrong. It wasn't the end of his jealous tantrums, it was just the beginning. When you accept something once, it's not that hard to accept it the second time. You might tell yourself things like, three strikes and he's out. But the third time may not be as bad as the second, so you might convince yourself that things are improving. At least that's what I did. I began to accept his jealously as part of the package, something we would deal with, get through. I told myself things like; no one's perfect, his good points outweigh his bad. I couldn't have imagined in my wildest dreams how dangerous he was. Occasionally I saw glimpses of something truly frightening in him, but with a snap of his fingers, his mask — the disguise he wore so comfortably — was back in place. I had no idea I was being methodically lured into his sick and dangerous trap. He was the predator and I was his prey.

Part II

Chapter 5

ONE SATURDAY EVENING in May we went to a dance club. We were dancing, laughing and hugging in between songs. I was having a good time. The deejay played a slow song and we waltzed, holding each other close. He kissed the top of my head and tightened his embrace. I looked up, smiled at him, then snuggled my head back against his shoulder. Suddenly I felt his hand slide between my legs. I stiffened and tried to push his hand away, he held it there forcefully.

"That's mine," he said in my ear.

"It's mine," I said forcefully. I pulled away and stomped across the floor, weaving around the other couples. I knew he was right behind me. I was angry, offended, and most of all disappointed in him. I got to our table, but before I could sit down he grabbed my wrist. I turned and faced him angrily. He glared at me. My stomach knotted as I yanked my wrist from his grip. "Let's go," he ordered. I walked as quickly as I could ahead of him focusing only on the fact I would soon be home, away from him. Once we were the in car, he told me I had humiliated him. I couldn't believe it.

"What are you talking about?' I snapped. "You humiliated me."

"There's nothing wrong with touching the person you love, it was an intimate moment," he stammered.

"That is so stupid," I said shaking my head.

"Are you calling me stupid?"

"What you're saying is stupid!"

"How dare you say I'm stupid, all I do for you and this is how you repay me?" He was whining like a spoiled child by now. I felt total disgust for him.

"What about the way you treated me on the dance floor, like I'm your property, like you have no respect for me, like you want to cheapen me," I choked the words out while fighting back tears.

"I don't have to cheapen you; you do a good job of that yourself. You and your fucking bands," he roared like a maniac. My emotions instantly transformed from strong and angry to weak and frightened. I sat there hating him as he raged on irrationally. "When two people love each other it's okay to touch in public. I'd love it if you touched me that way, at least I'd know you wanted the world to know we're together. I'm proud to be with you but you're not proud to be with me. How do you think that makes me feel? I've had it with your bullshit, and I mean it!"

I stared out the window thinking he was the biggest asshole I'd ever met. I felt some relief when he turned onto my street. He stopped the car abruptly in front of my building. I swung open the car door and started to get out. I only had one leg out of the vehicle when he started driving away. I had to grab the door handle to stop myself from falling out face first. He came to a squealing stop and told me to hurry up. I moved as fast as I possibly could. I barely got the door shut behind me when he screeched away. My heart was pounding fiercely as I made my way up the stairs. Once inside my apartment I calmed down a little. I felt utterly drained. I went directly to the bathroom and started running water for a bath. I undressed quickly and climbed into the tub before it was even half full. I sat listening to the sound of the running water and watching it fill the tub. The two scenes of slamming car doors and screeching tires played through my mind like a video — like a bad B movie. With a sigh, I realized I might be spending a lot of time in the bath tub if I stayed with this temperamental guy.

I'm not sure how long I'd been soaking in the hot water, and in self-pity, when I heard the phone ring. I cringed. He didn't leave a message, which made me feel uneasy. Just as I climbed from the tub and draped myself in a towel, the phone rang again. I answered on the fourth ring.

"What?" I said.

"Do you hate me?" he asked, sounding like a victim.

"No," I said stiffly, even though I did hate him that night.

"Do you love me?" I was astounded at his sudden change of tone. He actually sounded playful.

"I'm too pissed off to talk to you right now, especially about love. I'll talk to you tomorrow. Good night, Joe." I slammed the phone down as hard as I could without breaking it then slid into my bed. It felt good to have it all to myself.

He phoned me early the next morning. I was awake but pretended he woke me up. He said he'd call back later. I made myself a cup of coffee and phoned my mom. We talked for quite awhile. She was excited because one of her sisters was coming to spend a few days with her. I hung up feeling energized by her zeal. I threw on a T-shirt and a pair of sweat pants then cleaned every inch of my apartment. Once satisfied it was spotless, I phoned Chad. We chatted happily about what was happening in his life, then I phoned Myla. We talked for close to an hour catching up on the latest news. She asked me how Joe was. I told her he was fine and changed the subject. As we talked, I couldn't help thinking that if her boyfriend ever behaved the way Joe had, I'd be horrified. I would have made it my mission to convince her to dump him. I felt the shame creeping in.

A few minutes after my phone conversations, I opened the balcony door. I took a deep breath of the lilac-scented breeze and instantly felt the soothing affect of the aroma. While standing there, I began to wonder why Joe hadn't called back. I had call waiting, so I would have known if he'd been trying to reach me. Instead of feeling relieved, I felt kind of alarmed, maybe even a little disappointed. *What the heck was wrong with me?*

I decided to walk to the corner store and buy a news paper. I wanted to keep busy, distracted from thinking too much about him. I was heading to my bedroom to change when I heard loud music coming from outside. I hurried back to the balcony to investigate. There in the parking lot was Joe. He was standing by his car with the car door open. His radio was blaring out the song, *My Girl*. As soon as he saw me he raised his arms towards the sky and, at the top of his lungs, started singing along with the radio.

"I'm serenading you," he yelled up at me after singing the chorus.

I couldn't help laughing. He was such a spectacle standing below my balcony like a modern-day Romeo. His stage was the parking lot, his spot light, the blazing sun. My heart melted. He bowed. I applauded.

"May I come up?" he implored, his hands clasped in a begging position.

"As long as you promise not to sing," I shouted back.

He walked into my apartment already apologizing. "I was wrong, dead wrong. I'm an idiot, a love sick idiot. I'm sorry, baby." He was practically breathless from the combination of running up the stairs and talking so fast. "I don't know what I was thinking, I wasn't thinking. I mean I wasn't thinking about your feelings. I was just in the moment then; I felt bad or rejected, I guess, because you were so angry, which you had a right to be. I was wrong; I'm sorry. I'm so sorry."

He sounded like a tape on fast forward — the way he had the first time he'd apologized so profusely. I stood in front of him and let him ramble for a few minutes. Finally I interrupted him and suggested he sit down. We sat at the dining room table. He sat at one end. I sat at the other. We talked all afternoon. I explained my frustration to him. He appeared to listen and to understand.

"We have a loving and exciting relationship, Joe, but I don't understand some of the things you do," I said. "You say you're scared I'll break up with you, then you do things that make me *want* to break up with you. I think you're intentionally sabotaging our relationship."

He looked worried. I wasn't sure if it was because of what I said or because he didn't know how to respond. He stood up and walked over to the window. He stood there for a minute or two looking outside. Suddenly he turned around and looked at me with a knowing grin on his face. He came back to the table and sat down. "You know something? You hit the nail on the head. I am trying to sabotage it." He made this confession with a satisfied expression.

"Wonderful!" I replied sarcastically. "That's very encouraging."

"No, no!" he protested, waving his hands in front of him. "I mean, I'm not trying to sabotage our relationship on purpose. It's more like an unconscious thing. Leah, my beautiful, sweet Leah, I'm so in love with you; you're perfect. I'm so scared you'll meet someone else. I mean you could have anyone you want. Deep down I think you're going to leave me sooner or later so I do things to get it over with." His nervousness energy made the words pour out of him. He sounded as though he had made a huge discovery.

"You're who I want to be with. When you're not acting crazy, that is. I am not perfect and I don't want to be perfect," I lectured.

"To me you're perfect," he insisted, smiling proudly at me.

"I can't live up to that Joe, no one can."

"I'm not perfect either," he pointed out.

His comment hit me. He was smart, attractive, incredibly romantic and attentive. I loved being with him. I loved the way he made me feel, most of the time, almost all of the time. Did I expect him to be perfect? Was he simply a very passionate man in every way? He said he was sorry, he took responsibility. He serenaded me.

"I don't expect you to be perfect but I do expect you to be respectful, even when you're angry. It's demeaning to be yelled at, scolded and put down. I'm not your property; you can't do whatever you want to me in the name of love," I said firmly.

"I know what you're saying is true. You're smart, you're beautiful and you're sexy as hell. I'm a lucky guy, I don't want to lose you and I'm not going to risk it by being an asshole."

We kissed and made up.

Later that evening we went out for dinner. On the way back to my apartment we picked up a movie he wanted me to see, *Son of the Morning Star*. It was about Colonel Custer, a man he greatly admired. While watching the video, he told me he and his ex-wife had taken a trip to Little Bighorn County in Montana to see Custer's last stand. He promised he would take me someday. I told him I would like that. "It would be interesting to learn more about Sitting Bull," I said.

"Custer's wife loved him unconditionally," he said, deep in thought.

"Well maybe she did. Women didn't have many choices back then," I said casually. I didn't want to get into any sort of discussion about it. I just wanted to point it out. He didn't seem to grasp what I said; he was engaged in his own thoughts.

Throughout our relationship he rented that movie again and again. Over time, I realized it was an obsession.

Chapter 6

O UR RELATIONSHIP CHANGED after the episode at the nightclub. He
was calmer and wanted to stay in more. That was fine with me;
I had become tired of going out almost every night. Saturdays
were our date night; we usually went to a nice restaurant for dinner. He
always asked for a corner or secluded table when he made reservations,
and he insisted I sit with my back facing the rest of the patrons. I knew
it was so other men couldn't see me, or me them. I didn't confront him
about it because it didn't seem that big of a deal, and if it made him feel
secure then it was better for me. Besides, I enjoyed our dinner dates.
Generally, we lingered over our drinks and appetizers and ordered our
entrée late in the evening. Once we finished eating he ordered us a glass
of Port and toasted me with a kooky love poem he made up. Throughout
the evening we chatted up a storm discussing current events or sharing
our past. It felt as though we were the best of friends.

Other evenings, when we hung out at my apartment, we watched
movies or just sat and talked. He often presented me with a hypothetical
situation then asked what I would do. One night he asked me if I would
tell him if I was ever attracted to someone else.

"Would you want to know?" I asked, then quickly added, "Because if
you were attracted to someone else, I wouldn't want to know. If you were
going to act on it, then I'd want to know."

"I couldn't be attracted to someone else; I'm in love with you. It's impossible, at least for me, maybe not for you." He was agitated and continued with a long tirade about honesty and the true meaning of love. He ended his boring lecture by saying, "When you love someone, you can't be attracted to other people, not if it's true love."

By this time, I was feeling more than just a little perturbed. "Okay, Joe," I said impatiently, "I get what you're saying. Why in the hell did you even ask the question?"

"Because I don't want to get hurt, I want to know the truth. If you're attracted to other guys I have a right to know," he replied, raising his voice slightly.

"I really don't appreciate being lectured on what true love is, especially after some of the shit you pulled on me," I snapped in frustration. "You're no expert on love, Joe."

He looked stunned by my reply. Then suddenly a big smile spread across his face. He stood up from his chair, walked over to me, knelt down and took my hand.

"I love you, and I don't have to be an expert to know that," he said decisively. He lifted my hand to his lips and kissed it.

I looked at him kneeling beside my chair, holding my hand and looking at me with tenderness. I let go of my frustration and smiled at him. "Good thing!" I said.

He rose and kind of chuckled. "You're a little spit fire," he said proudly.

He often talked about his daughter, Alexandra. She lived in New York with Lisa, her mom. He said Lisa moved there after they split up and eventually married an American. He claimed he kept in close touch with Alexandra and saw her as often as he could, but that Lisa made it very difficult for him. He claimed she was bitter because he wouldn't marry her when she got pregnant. "I couldn't marry her; I didn't love her," he explained. "I think she got pregnant on purpose, but it doesn't matter. I love my daughter."

He told me he went to New York just before he met me. "I was there for two weeks and saw my little girl once. I've spent a fortune on lawyers and finally decided that instead of spending all my money on lawyers I'd put it into an education fund for her. I phone her once a week and I'll see her when I can. I don't want to confuse her." He was always emotional when he spoke about Alexandra.

He also talked about Julie, his second wife, a lot. He often said he wished he had never married her because she was crazy and lied about everything. One day he said, "Seriously, Leah, she's nuts. When I told her I wanted a divorce, she tried to commit suicide. She took a bunch of pills and blamed it on me. I stayed with her for a couple more months after that, but finally I couldn't take it anymore. I had to get away from her. She said she would get even with me. Thank God she moved to Florida, I hope she never comes back."

"So, have all your exes fled the country?" I joked. He didn't seem amused.

Whenever he'd ask me questions about my ex-husband and our marriage, he acted disappointed with my answers. "If your marriage was so great, why did you get a divorce?" he asked.

"Obviously it wasn't great. As I told you before, he has a drinking problem and he cheated on me. I was heartbroken for a long time, but I'm over it. I moved on a long time ago. Now I think of him as my children's father and I'm not going to slam my children's father." I said. "Not saying I never have, but I don't anymore. I think he's a better person than he used to be, and so am I for that matter."

I knew he felt threatened because I didn't hate or even dislike my ex-husband, and I resented that. Also, I hated the way he talked about his ex-wife. It was vindictive.

Chapter 7

BY THE END of June I had become very unhappy with some things at work. I told Joe, probably out of frustration more than anything, that I wanted to work as an independent agent. I explained I could work from home. The idea excited him so much I had to calm him down.

"It's not something I can rush into. I have to be prepared; there's a lot involved here," I explained.

"Leah, trust me," he said, putting his hand over his heart. "I'll help you. You can do this."

His enthusiasm was contagious and unstoppable. He got involved. He found me a great deal on a fax machine and a photocopier. Together we converted my spare room into an office. By the end of July I had my contracts printed, my files set up, and a modest clientele. I had my own business. I was scared, yet determined. Most of the bands I'd been representing had signed a contract with the agency, which meant I'd have to look for new acts. I knew that would take time. Fortunately, Terry's band had not renewed their contract with the agency and wanted to continue working with me. They were one of the best, if not *the* best club acts in western Canada. When I told Joe the wonderful news he smiled. But I could see it was a fake smile.

I was so busy all through August, it was a bit of a blur. I often had to go out and see acts I heard were looking for an agent. Joe accompanied me. He was gracious when meeting these groups and interested in my opinion of their performances. I always asked him what he thought of them as well. He'd basically agree with whatever my opinion was.

One morning I got a call from a fellow named Guy Cool. He was looking for an agent to represent his band. The name of the band was The Cool Guys, which made me chuckle. He said he had been booking the band himself because they had been playing only local venues, but now they wanted to go on the road. He also told me Terry had recommended me. I called Terry after talking to Guy and thanked him for the recommendation.

"You'll like them, Leah, they're a strong act, and Guy is a fantastic front man," he said. "As you know, I have the week off. I'd be glad to go with you to see them."

"That'd be fun," I responded.

"How about tonight?"

I agreed without hesitation.

As soon as I hung up the phone, sensibility set in. I knew Joe would have a jealous tantrum if I told him I was meeting Terry. I didn't want to invite him to come along, it would be too stressful. I suddenly resented Joe so much it felt like hatred. I decided I was going, and I wasn't going to tell him who I was going with or where I was going.

As the day went on, I started feeling as guilty as hell. I wondered how I would feel if it was the other way around. I began to have second thoughts, but at the same time I knew I wasn't doing anything wrong. Terry and I had been friends for years. I valued our friendship and didn't want to lose it over Joe's jealousy issues. I told myself Joe would get over it, eventually, but for now it was best to keep my friendship with Terry away from him. I phoned Joe and told him I was going to go shopping with Myla. I felt childish lying to him. *He's put you this position.*

"What time will you be home?" he asked in a sulky voice.

"I have no idea," I said, annoyed by his tone.

"Well, are you going to be late?"

"I don't think so."

"I guess I'll call a couple buddies and go out for a beer."

"That's a good idea," I replied. *Please don't go to the same place I'm going.* I wasn't too worried that would happen. I was going to a neighbourhood pub miles away from where he lived. I figured it was unlikely he'd even heard of the place.

It took me a while to relax once I got to the pub. I greeted Terry in what I hoped seemed a natural way, but I was nervous Joe would come pouncing in and make a scene. I despised feeling that way and actually managed to convince myself my mind was exaggerating. I forced myself to focus my attention on the band, and I was impressed. I thanked Terry for recommending me to them. I was especially impressed with Guy Cool. He had a powerful voice and great stage presence. He was also young and good looking, which is a definite perk in the music business. The band finished their set then came over and joined us. Guy was as eager to discuss business with me as I was with him. He told me what they expected money wise. It was a reasonable request. I knew once they got known in the circuit they would make a lot more than he expected. We shook hands on the agreement that I would represent them exclusively. It was so easy. I was thrilled. I bought a round of drinks for everyone.

As soon as the band left our table to play their second set, Terry raised his glass of beer. He was grinning from ear to ear. "Congratulations, Miss Super Agent."

"Thanks, Terry. I couldn't have done it without you," I said with a grateful smile. "You're such a good friend."

The band started to play a ballad. Terry stood up and asked me to dance while reaching out for my hand. It felt strange holding his hand and walking to the dance floor. I had never danced with him before. He was a good dancer, easy to follow. I was a little surprised by how I felt being so close to him. It wasn't as though I'd never been attracted to him before, but I had never encouraged anything. I didn't date clients. His hand stayed firmly on the middle of my back as he lowered his shoulders and snuggled a little closer to me. I didn't resist. The song ended and we sat down. After a few seconds of awkward silence, Terry began talking. He told me he and the rest of his band wanted to come off the road.

"I'm forty years old, Leah. I have a sixteen-year-old son who I don't spend enough time with. My ex-wife called me a few days ago. She's worried about him; his attitude and stuff. I felt bad." He spoke as though thinking out loud.

"It's the right thing to do, Terry," I said looking at him warmly.

"Maybe I'll find a good woman and settle down," he said, giving me a smile and a mischievous wink.

I smiled back at him. "You're growing up so fast," I teased. He laughed.

"So, are you still going out with serious Joe?"

I chuckled a bit and nodded. "Is Guy Cool his real name?" I asked, to change the subject.

"I'm pretty sure it is," Terry said, raising his eyebrows as if to say, how about that!

I ended up staying longer than I had planned to. I was having too much fun to go home. Terry was hilarious; I loved his sense of humour. When I finally did decide to head home, Terry walked me to my car. He gave me a hug goodnight, a long hug. I drove home thinking about him. I tried to push aside the thoughts about dancing with him, about hugging him. I promised myself I wouldn't lose touch with him if the band ever stopped performing.

When I turned into the parking lot of my building, I noticed a car at the edge of the lot. It was beyond the range of the street light, so all I could make out was that it was white. Joe drove a white car. I shuddered at the thought he might be waiting for me. I drove slowly into the underground parking area, checking my rear view mirror to make sure no one was following me. I got into my apartment and went directly to the living room window to peer outside. I couldn't see if the car was still there. I told myself I was just being paranoid then checked my phone messages. Not surprisingly, there were two from Joe. He had left the first message at ten o'clock, requesting I call him as soon as I got home. The second message was to tell me not to phone him because he was going to bed. He had left that at eleven o'clock. He sounded discouraged.

Chapter 8

WHEN JOE CALLED the next morning I expected him to question me about the night before. He didn't. He didn't even ask me what time I got home. I was pleasantly surprised, maybe even a little shocked. I told myself it was a good sign.

"Good morning baby," he greeted brightly.

"Good morning," I replied softly.

"I'm just heading out to work."

"I'm just heading in to work," I said, smiling to myself.

"Do you have a busy day ahead of you?"

"Yes. I have a new band to book."

"That's good," he replied. "It's going to be hot outside today. What do you think about going to a nice air-conditioned restaurant for dinner tonight?"

"I think that's a good idea," I said happily.

"You pick the spot. I'll be there to pick you up at, say, six-thirty."

Off and on throughout the day, I wondered if he was saving all his questions for later. I rehearsed my story a few times. I hated feeling so deceitful.

I faxed the only copy I had of The Cool Guy's promo package to several clubs then got on the phone and did my sales pitch on the band. By four o'clock I had three weeks booked for them. I phoned Guy and discussed the contracts. He wanted to come over right away and sign them. He lived quite a long way from me.

"You're going to hit rush hour traffic this time of day," I said. "Why don't you drop by tomorrow instead?"

"That would probably be better," he said a little reluctantly.

"If you come over in the afternoon, I'll probably have another booking for you." He seemed happy with that arrangement and said he would call in the morning to set up a time.

I was exhausted, which was the main reason I didn't want him to come over. I turned my answering machine on and went for a nap. I slept for about forty minutes then got up and checked my phone messages. Terry had left a message simply asking me to call him when I had a chance. Joe had also called. His message sounded frantic. I called him.

"Where were you?" he asked. I told him I'd had a nap. "Did you have a late night last night?" he questioned.

"No, I had a busy day though and it's so hot in here," I said nonchalantly. He replied, in a grumpy voice, that he'd had a busy day too. I brushed off his attitude and said I was looking forward to seeing him. He perked up a bit.

After an extra long shower and a can of cold pop, I felt energized. I curled my hair with the curling iron then put my favourite sundress on. Joe arrived twenty minutes early.

"Wow! I like your hair," he said the second I opened the door. "You should wear it like that more often."

I smiled and thanked him. He looked me over as he strode in. "It *is* hot in here, but not as hot as you, Leah." My spirits were quickly raised.

"You're pretty hot yourself."

He slid his arms around my waist and held me close, whispering, "I love you."

"I love you too."

At the restaurant we lingered over dinner. He was talkative and funny. I wondered how I could have questioned my feelings for him. He was amazing. So what if he was jealous. It was nothing compared to his charm. I was so lucky.

When we got back to my place a cool breeze was blowing through the open window. He said he wanted to stay with me until I fell asleep, then he was going home because he had a meeting early the next morning. It was only ten o'clock and I wasn't tired. I suggested he go home and get a good night's sleep.

"Why are you trying to get rid of me?" he asked seriously.

"I'm not trying to get rid of you," I laughed.

"I just want to make sure you're safe and sound before I leave," he explained, running his finger down my arm. We were in bed minutes later. He fell asleep before I did. I woke him up at midnight. He sleepily asked me to set the alarm for five then turned on his side and went back to sleep. I set the alarm then curled up next to him and dozed off. When the alarm rang, he jumped out of bed as if it was a fire drill. He was gone in minutes. I stretched out and fell back to sleep. A couple of hours later, I woke up from a horrible dream — a nightmare. I sat up in bed shaken by the graphic images left in my head.

I was running down the stairs of my apartment building. I was covered in blood. My legs were wobbly and I thought I was going to fall. Joe was right behind me, I couldn't see him but I could hear him and feel his wrath. He was going to kill me. I tried to scream but nothing would come out. I could see Terry outside the glass doors at the bottom of the stairs. He was running across the parking lot to help me when a car ran into him. He flew into the air and disappeared.

I spent most of the morning trying to analyse it. In my dream, Terry disappeared. Was I afraid once the band broke up I wouldn't see Terry anymore? Was I afraid Joe would make Terry disappear? Was my subconscious telling me Joe is dangerous, a monster? I talked myself out of believing that.

I returned Terry's call from the day before. I felt uncomfortable talking to him at first, but his relaxed mannerism soon put me at ease. He said he was looking forward to coming off the road and hoped I would be able to find him plenty of local venues. I felt a surge of relief after talking to him. It was perfect; Terry and his band coming off the road opened a space for Guy and his band. Guy going on the road opened a space for Terry and his band in the local circuit. It was the first time I truly believed my little, home-based business was going to make it. I felt inspired.

It was noon when Guy Cool showed up to see me. While he was there I confirmed a fourth week for the band. He sat across from my desk smiling. "That was fun," he said, "listening to you promote the band and seal the deal. Obviously the buyer trusts you." He smiled at me. I felt a little self conscious about being appraised.

"I just tell the truth," I said shrugging my shoulders.

"Terry said you were a good agent, and he was right," he said grinning and slanting his head a little. I felt myself blushing.

"Oh stop it," I said, flicking my wrist at him. He let out a relaxed little laugh.

I knew I was very lucky to be representing The Cool Guys. I walked him to the door, we shook hands and said goodbye. I had barely shut the door when my buzzer rang. It was Joe. I wasn't expecting him. I buzzed him in then jogged over to my living room window and checked outside. I saw Guy in the parking lot unlocking the door to his car, which was parked right beside Joe's. They must have passed each other in the door-way. My phone rang as I was letting Joe in, so I scooted back to my office to answer it. He strolled into my office and sat down while I chatted with a client. He was dressed in a shirt and tie. His olive skin glowed next to the stark, white shirt. I smiled at him approvingly. He smiled back then loosened his tie. I rushed through my phone conversation.

"You look nice," I said, hanging up the phone.

"Thanks. It's been a long, nerve-wracking morning. I'm dealing with an idiot," he said shaking his head in disgust. "I need a drink."

"I don't have anything," I said crinkling my nose.

"Have you had lunch?"

"Not yet."

"Then let me take you out."

"Okay, but I don't want to be gone too long. I have a lot to do," I said firmly. I was wearing jeans and a tank top. "Maybe I should change since you're all dressed up."

"You look gorgeous," he said. "Here, I'll take my tie off." He pulled it up over his head then hurried into the bathroom and fixed his hair. I laughed and told him he was worse than a woman.

We were walking to his car, hand in hand, when a car pulled up. It was Guy. He sprang from his car. I saw a large envelope in his hand. "Leah," he shouted, making his way towards us. He nodded his head and smiled at Joe. I could feel Joe's tension. I squeezed his hand. "Hi," I greeted awkwardly.

"I was half way home before I realized I didn't give you our promo package," he explained, handing me the thick envelope. I quickly introduced him to Joe. "Nice to meet you," Guy said, extending his hand. Much to my relief, Joe shook his hand and smiled politely.

"Guy's the leader of the new band I told you about," I explained. Joe shrugged as though he didn't know what I was talking about.

He didn't say a word as we drove to the restaurant. I occupied myself by humming along to the song on the radio and promising myself if he threw another tantrum that would be it. He pulled into the parking lot of a Chinese restaurant. Once the car was stopped he turned to me.

"So, that Guy fellow is pretty good looking." He looked at me as if he was studying my face for evidence.

"He's not bad. The band is good, really good," I replied, hoping he wouldn't ask me how I knew them. He did. "They're a local band, been around for a long time," I said, indicating I thought he should have known that. His mood changed instantly and he announced he was starving. I relaxed.

While we were eating, he told me all about his meeting with the manager of a gym. He referred to the guy as the idiot. "He wants me to collect money from customers who didn't sign contracts," he said, tapping his finger on his temple and crossing his eyes. We both laughed. Time flew by. It was quarter to three when he dropped me off.

"Don't work too hard, Princess Leah," he shouted out his car window as I was walking up the sidewalk to the door of my building.

"I won't, Joe Skywalker," I shouted back.

The next few weeks flew by. Between work and Joe, I barely had a moment to myself. One evening he arrived at my apartment and announced he had a surprise for me. He was holding a dozen red roses, a bag of groceries and a bottle of wine. He had told me earlier he wanted to cook dinner but wouldn't tell me what he was planning on making. He insisted I stay out of the kitchen while he cooked. I occupied myself by getting dressed, painting my toenails and fussing with my hair. It was fun to get dressed up for dinner in my own home. I put on the faded blue-jean skirt and white tank top I'd bought earlier in the week. When I came out of my room, Joe was setting the table. He turned and looked at me. His face lit up. He put his hand over his heart and gave me one of his favourite lines. "Be still my heart." I laughed and walked into his open arms.

"You're so sexy," he said taking a deep breath. He had closed all the drapes and lit candles. I told him whatever he was cooking smelled amazing. He pulled a chair out for me to sit down then served dinner. He had made chicken breasts stuffed with rice and mushroom and covered with a creamy cheese sauce. Each bite melted in my mouth. He looked so proud when I complimented him. He said it was his mom's recipe.

"I love it," I said.

"I love you."

"I love you too."

"You look beautiful in the candlelight," he said softly, his eyes looking deeply into mine. I felt warm, loved and safe. After we ate, he went to his jacket and pulled a small square box out of his pocket. It was wrapped in silver paper. He led me over to the couch and gently pulled me down on his knee. "This for you, baby," he said handing it to me. I opened it slowly and gasped when I saw the shiny, gold bracelet. It was exquisite. He put it on my wrist.

"Thank you so much, Joe." I was feeling so overcome my eyes filled up with tears.

"You're welcome. You deserve to have nice things, Princess," he said while he stroked my hair. I cuddled up against his shoulder and we sat like that for a long time.

A few weeks later we went to Banff for the weekend. It was nice to escape from the big concrete jungle and spend a few days in the mountains. We stayed at a luxurious hotel with a swimming pool. Late in the evening, when we could have the pool to ourselves, we went for long, relaxing, playful swim. He told he would buy me a house with a pool some day. The next morning we called room service and ordered breakfast. While we were waiting for our meal he told me he wanted to move in with me. He said he wanted to wake up beside me every morning.

"We're not kids trying to find ourselves; we know who we are and what we want. I know I want to be with you for the rest of my life," he said, holding my hand and looking lovingly into my eyes.

I was reluctant in some ways, and in other ways I liked the idea. We were together most of the time anyway. I thought perhaps he would feel more secure if we were living together. A voice inside me warned me not to do it. I argued with the voice, reasoned with it, then ignored it. I was so sure I was loved and in love.

Chapter 9

H E MOVED IN with me the first Sunday in September. He brought his furniture with him. We moved my couch and a couple of end tables into the office and took the rest of my furniture into the large storage room off the hallway. I was surprised how much it bothered me to see his furniture replace mine. His was newer and more expensive, but I liked mine more and it bugged me he didn't think it was good enough for him. I also felt as if he was taking over. I told myself I was being silly and I should enjoy the change.

The first few days after he moved in were like a honeymoon. I noticed a shift in him on the Friday evening. He came home from work while I was on the phone. When I finished the conversation I came out of my office to greet him. He was sitting in the living room watching the television.

"Hi," I chirped as I bent down and kissed him on the cheek.

"Hi," he mumbled, staring straight ahead at the television.

"Is something wrong?"

"Usually you meet me at the door when I come home. Today you ignored me," he whined.

"I was on the phone doing business," I said impatiently.

"Were you talking to Jeff Cool?"

I started laughing. "I think you mean Guy Cool, and no that's not who I was talking to. I was talking to Joan Roberts, the manager of a club in Edmonton."

He was cold and quiet all evening. I didn't bother asking him what was wrong. I figured if he was pouting because I didn't meet him at the door, that was his problem. I still hadn't learned; his problems were my problems.

The next morning while I was making the bed, he stood in the doorway watching me. He started criticizing the way I was tucking in the sheets. "I know how to make a bed, Joe," I snapped. He yelled so loud I jumped. "Bullshit!"

"Then you make it," I said, feeling myself close to tears. He went into a raging rant. He rambled on so fast I barely caught what he was saying. I just wanted to get away from him. I tried walking out of the room, but he grabbed my arm and swung me around to face him. His grip was tight. I ordered him to let go of me. He squeezed harder. "You're hurting me," I told him. I was frightened. He shoved me away with enough force to knock me against the wall. I was physically and emotionally stunned. I heard him muttering to himself as he stormed out of the apartment. I went to the window and watched him drive off.

I was relieved he was gone, but I knew he'd be back before the end of the day. I couldn't think straight. I wanted to throw his clothes over the balcony. I wanted him out. I had this sick feeling that it didn't matter what I wanted. I sat down heavily and stared into space. I was scared of him. I realized I had been scared for a long time; I just had not wanted to admit it. I prayed it wasn't true. I prayed he wouldn't act that way ever again. An eerie loneliness came over me. I stood up, walked back into the bedroom and finished making the bed. I tried to rehearse what I would say to him when he got back, but I couldn't put my thoughts together in a sensible way. I flopped down on the bed and cried. Before long, I was scolding myself. *You shouldn't have let him move in. What's wrong with you, Leah?*

A couple of hours had passed when I heard his key in the door. By then, I was lying on the couch watching an old movie. I sat up, tensing. He came into the living room with a bouquet of red roses in one hand and a bottle of wine in the other. He handed both to me. I took them without saying a word then went into the kitchen, put the wine away and placed the flowers in a vase. He leaned against the counter and watched me.

"I'm sorry Leah," he said in a soft, almost frightened voice.

"What are you sorry for, Joe?" I asked sternly. I wanted him to admit what he'd done.

"For the way I acted, the way I treated you."

"Because you didn't like the way I was making the bed!" The words exploded from my mouth. "You threw a violent tantrum over something that minor. What is wrong with you?"

"I'm not perfect, sweetheart. I do have a bad temper and I'm working on it."

"I'm not perfect either, Joe, no one is, but yelling and shoving is a little more than just not being perfect. You can control your temper, so don't use that excuse. You have no idea how upset I am. I'm so disappointed in you. I want to kick you out!" I was yelling and fighting back tears. I saw his face redden then tears form in his eyes. He shuffled into the living room and sat down. I waited a few minutes then went to see what he was doing. He was sitting slouched over with his head in his hands, sobbing. I watched him for a few seconds. I had never seen a man cry like that. Finally, I couldn't stand it any longer. I went over and sat down on the arm of the chair. "Calm down," I said as I rubbed his back. He looked up at me then went through his now familiar display of remorse. "Please forgive me Leah. I'm begging you." He looked frightened and small; nothing like the person I had seen earlier.

"I forgive you," I said, uncertain whether I really meant it. He promised me I wouldn't regret it.

The next day Chad and Myla came over for dinner. He fused over them like a grandma. We had a lovely evening with great food and good conversation. Before they left he did up a plate of leftovers for them to take home. I was sure I was seeing the real Joe. The incident from the previous day paled in comparison.

A little while after the kids left we began cleaning up the kitchen. I turned the stereo up loud and sang along to the REM song, *Man on the Moon*. Joe didn't know the words. Instead of singing, "If you believe they put a man on the moon," he sang, "If you believe they shot a man on the moon." I laughed and corrected him. Then he started singing, "They put Stan on the moon, Stan on the moon." I laughed at his silliness.

A couple of days later Carrie came over. I showed her the changes in the living room and waited for her reaction.

"Wow, this is pretty fancy furniture," she said, scouting the room with her eyes.

"I know. A little on the pretentious side though. I prefer more of an earthy look, as you know. Check out those brass ornaments," I said pointing to the fireplace mantel. "I hate them." Carrie laughed then suggested I tell him I didn't like them. "I will eventually, it's just that he's so proud of them. I guess I can deal with them for a little while."

"It doesn't look like your home anymore," she said sadly.

"It doesn't feel like my home anymore. I didn't expect to feel this way, but I do. Everything happened too fast. I miss living alone, I miss my furniture, I miss my old job and the people I worked with. What the hell was I thinking?" I was surprised by my outburst but relieved I had admitted my true feelings.

"Is everything okay?"

"Yeah, I just have some adjusting to do. I've been single for a long time."

I poured us each a cup of coffee and I told her I was concerned we had rushed into living together.

"You're not obligated, Leah. It's okay to change your mind," she said in a motherly tone. I nodded in agreement. I didn't want to tell her about his temper tantrums; it was too embarrassing. I knew I couldn't explain it without sounding crazy. I dropped the topic and we went on to discuss other things.

Two hours later she decided she should head home. Before she left she proposed that the four of us get together on the weekend. She said she and Ken wanted to get to know Joe better. I liked the idea of hanging out with them and couldn't help hoping Ken's easy going disposition would rub off on Joe. When he got home from work I approached him with Carrie's suggestion. I was actually a little surprised by his willingness to go out with them.

The four of us went out for dinner the following weekend. Joe was witty and charming. Ken, as usual, was hilarious and had all of us bent over laughing several times. At one point during the evening Joe announced he was going to marry me. I nearly choked on my food.

"Have you set a date?" Carrie asked, glancing at me with an amused grin.

"Not yet," Joe said, sliding his arm over my shoulder. After a few seconds of awkward silence Ken told a funny joke and made everyone laugh. Then Joe told a joke just as funny and looked pleased when he got the same response.

Later, at home, Joe said, "Remember what I said in the restaurant, that I'm going to marry you someday?"

"Yes, I remember. You caught me off guard."

"I'd marry you tomorrow," he admitted eagerly.

"You shouldn't be telling my friends we're getting married, we haven't even talked about it. I'm not in a hurry to get married, Joe. As we both know, it's not something anyone should rush into."

"True, but I *am* going to marry you someday." His tone indicated his decision was not open to discussion.

Chapter 10

H E CAME HOME from work early one day. I was in my office when I heard him unlocking the door. I went to the doorway to greet him. He looked at me strangely. "You look like the cat that ate the canary," he huffed.

I ignored his absurd comment and asked him why he was home so early. He stomped past me without answering; poured himself a drink, went into the living room, sat down and lit a cigarette. I went back to my office, but I couldn't concentrate on my work. I was insulted by the way he had treated me and knew I couldn't relax unless I confronted him. I put my paperwork away and went out to the living room. He seemed to be waiting for me.

"Did you have a bad day, Joe?" I said, unconsciously placing my hand on my hip.

"You're my bad day," he shouted, glaring hatefully at me. My heart sank.

"You don't give a shit do you?" he spat.

"What are you talking about?"

"What time did you get up this morning?"

"About eight," I said, resenting the question, resenting him.

"About eight," he mocked. "I got up at six. I'm the only guy at work whose wife doesn't get up and make him breakfast or at least a cup of cof-fee. How the fuck do you think that makes me feel? All I do for you and you're too fucking selfish to do a little thing like that for me!" His voice rose louder with each word.

"You told me you can't eat that early in the morning," I said defensively. *What an asshole, what an asshole, what an asshole!*

He stood up, pointed his finger at me and shouted, "You fucking lying bitch." His cruel words felt like a punch in the face. I gasped for air. He sat back down and dived into his rage. "I've had it with you. Look at this furniture, my furniture. Do you know what this cost me?" He waited for an answer. I just shook my head because I was too scared to tell him I didn't give a shit. "Thousands of dollars and I bring it to you because all you have is a bunch of junk."

"It's not junk to me," I retorted. I was nervous, hurt and angry. I told myself if he didn't shut up I was walking out the door. *I'll go to Carrie's and spend the night.*

"You like junk because you have no fucking class. You probably fucked that pretty boy Guy Cool that morning he was here. You fucking slut. I'll find out for sure, I have my ways. I know people, Leah. People who can make you disappear." His eyes were piercing through me. I felt sick to my stomach.

"I'm leaving," I announced loudly. I stood up, marched into the bedroom, grabbed my purse and headed for the door. Mentally, I planned to phone him from Carrie's and tell him to pack his belongings and get the hell out of my house. My eyes were burning with tears. I couldn't wait to get away from him.

I was only half way across the room when he sprang off the chair and rushed towards me. Before I could move away he put me in a head lock and dragged me back into the living room. *Oh God, he's going to hurt me.* He kicked the back of my legs and knocked me to the floor. I was terrified. I tried to get up. He knocked me back, and I moaned loudly. He was soon straddling me and pinning my arms down with his knees. I couldn't believe what was happening; it didn't seem real; it didn't seem possible. I rolled my body back and forth in panic. I yelled at him to get off. He belted me across the face over and over again. I was crying hysterically. "Shut up!" he roared. I kept crying out. He covered my mouth with his hand and pressed until I could taste blood. "If you don't shut up I'll knock your teeth out," he threatened, his eyes wild and crazy. I tried to stifle my sobs. He held his fist up. I closed my eyes. "Shut up!" he yelled again. I shut up. I lay there, helpless under his weight, feeling terrified. I began to pray as he viciously slapped my face and head again and again. *God please make him stop.*

Finally he got off me, grabbed my wrists and pulled me up. My legs felt wobbly, I was dizzy and disoriented. Nothing seemed real. I was in a state of shock. I had lost track of time. He grabbed me by the hair, pulled me across the room then shoved me onto the couch. I landed face first. He left me there while he went into the kitchen to make another drink. He brought me a drink too. I took it with shaky hands and drank it fast. I didn't know what to do. I just sat there frozen.

"Fuck you're stupid," he growled.

I stared at a magazine sitting on the coffee table in front of me and tried to focus. I could feel him scowling at me. The only thing that was real to me was the date on the magazine; October 1994. I spelled October in my head.

"Go wash your face," he suddenly commanded. "You're a fucking mess."

I told myself to do what he said. I shut the bathroom door and looked in the mirror. My face looked like raw meat. I touched it gently. My eyes were bloodshot and rimmed with mascara. I rubbed eye makeup remover over them, wiped them with a tissue then stared at my reflection. It didn't look like me; it looked like a battered woman. Tears poured from my eyes. *It's not true; it can't be true. I've been fooling myself; he'll never change, he doesn't want to change, I'm terrified of him.*

I composed myself as much as I could before coming out of the bathroom. My first instinct was to go into the bedroom and slam the door, but an image of him attacking me in the bedroom flashed through my head. Reluctantly, I walked back to the living room. He was on the phone talking to someone in Italian. I heard him say whore in plain English a couple times. He hung up and looked at me as though I was one big disappointment. I was sitting on the couch smoking a cigarette because I wanted to do something I hadn't been ordered to do. It was all sinking in; I was horrified and outraged by my predicament. I looked at him the same way he was looking at me.

"Dominique is mad at me because of you," he sneered. "I told him about you having guys over when I'm not home. You know what he said? He said I better get rid of you or he will.

Before I could stop myself I said defiantly, "I have a couple friends who would say the same thing if I told them what you did to me." I couldn't keep my mouth shut, I just couldn't. I had to try to hang on to the tiny shreds of dignity I had left. But then I started to get really worried. I had never met Dominique, and I didn't want to. Joe had told me many stories about this man. When we were dating, he told me Dominique was a successful business man who lived in Seattle, Washington, and owned a chain of hotels across the United States. He said they had met in Vancouver, at a party, and became instant friends. He described Dominique as a handsome man in his mid sixties who lived in a mansion and owned a yacht. He claimed he had spent a lot of time in Seattle with this wealthy friend and that he thought of the older man as a father, more of a father than his own. Shortly after he moved in with me he told me Dominique had mafia connections and was a powerful man. I was horrified and told him I wanted nothing to do with criminals. He laughed and said he was just kidding. After that he'd often imply that he knew a lot about organized crime. I'd merely change the subject, or try to; I didn't want him to think for a minute I was impressed. I even suggested he watched too many mafia movies. He said he only watched them if they were realistic.

I lost track of time again and was startled out of my reverie by Joe's sudden laugh. It was as though he knew what I was thinking about. "You have no idea who my friends are and what they're capable of. You better be very careful, Leah, or you'll bring a whole lot of misery to your friends." He looked at me as if daring me to say something. His crazy eyes backed me down. I looked away. *You're a freak, a crazy, pathetic freak.*

He sat in silence for a while. Then out of the blue he started to cry. The next thing I knew he was grumbling about his parents taking him away from his aunt. I was weak with relief to see that his fit of fury was over, but I couldn't believe, after what he had just done, he had the gall to sit there crying over something that happened more than thirty years ago. I sat listening to him cry and complain that his aunt was the only woman who had never hurt him. I was so angry I wanted to scream at the top of my lungs, tell him to get out of my house, tell him I didn't blame his parents for sending him away, tell him I wished I could send him away.

"You hurt me," I sternly reminded him. He looked at me as if he'd forgotten what he had done. I gazed at his puffy eyes and tearstained face. I silently promised myself I'd find a way to get him the hell out of my life. I had to.

"I don't know why I hurt you, I love you. I'd rather die than lose you. You have to believe me, Leah, I'm so sorry. Oh my sweet, beautiful, Princess Leah, I'm so sorry. "Please don't leave me. Please give me another chance."

I stared blankly at him, hardly able to believe his abrupt mood change and his snivelling pleas for forgiveness. "Stop it, Joe. You hit me. You beat me. Now you expect me just to let it go. Do you think I'm going to live like this?"

"No, I know you won't live like this. I don't want you to. It's not going happen again," he said frantically. He was leaning forward in the chair trying to make eye contact with me.

"I've heard that before," I snapped.

"I know, but this was really bad. I learned a lesson," he said as if the experience had been successful because he learned a lesson. I couldn't help wonder if he had really learned a lesson or if I had been taught a lesson. "I had no idea I could lose it like that," he continued. "It's never happened before and it will never happen again. I don't know, Leah, I think I love you too much. It scares me. I hate it. I just want to relax and be happy. I don't want to hurt you, Leah. I swear on my life, I'll never hurt you again. I don't blame you if you break up with me, I deserve it. But if you can find it in your heart to forgive me, I won't let you down."

"You knocked me to the floor, sat on me, slapped me over and over again; you pulled me across the room by my hair. That is not love!" I yelled. I was outraged by his lame excuses. I'd never been so full of hatred and disgust in my life. Such horrible feelings, yet I was relieved by them.

"I love you more than my first breath, Leah. You have to believe that. You know I love you. You never have to doubt it. I doubt your love for me all the time. That's why I'm so scared." He was crying again. It was useless.

I hardly listened to his ramblings. I had heard these protestations too many times; I no longer believed him. Feeling sure his anger was completely spent, and that I was no longer in danger, I told him I was going to have a bath. I desperately needed some time alone. It was now ten o'clock. This nightmare had been going on for five gruelling hours.

"Do you want me to wash your back?" he asked sweetly.

I silenced the angry voice inside me that wanted to verbally assault him and calmly told him I wanted to be alone and relax.

So many thoughts struggled for my attention while I soaked in the hot water. I couldn't relax. I could feel his presence. I clasped my hands together in front of me. "Please God, make him go away," I prayed.

When I finally got out of the tub I went directly to my bedroom. I wanted to go to bed and escape into sleep, but the thought of him climbing in beside me stopped me. I dressed quickly then heard him coming down the hallway. I jumped when he swung open the door and sulkily asked me to come and have a glass of wine with him.

"I'll be right out," I mumbled sounding as gloomy as I felt.

"Don't be long," he said impatiently.

Drop dead.

As soon as I sat down on the couch he brought me a glass of wine then sat down next to me. He put his arm around me and kissed the side of my head. I pulled away and asked him for a cigarette. The packet was on a table across the room. He got up to get it. When he sat back down he left a small space between us. "I love you," he whispered as he lit my cigarette. "I'm going to make this up to you. You'll see. In time it will be like it never happened." He sounded confident.

"I will never forget what happened, Joe." I assured him. "This is serious."

"I know. I wish I could take all back. I'll never forgive myself, never," he said nervously.

"So how do you expect me to forgive you?" I asked, actually thinking I was challenging him.

"I would forgive you no matter what you did because I love you."

"I would never do what you did, to anyone," I said feeling a sense of superiority over him. I took a big gulp of my wine.

"If you did, I would forgive you. That's love, Leah," he said as tears started flowing down his face again. "You're the best thing that's ever happened to me, and I won't let you go. You can't leave me." His shoulders were slumped forward and his face twisted with pain. He got up, went into the bathroom and blew his nose. Seconds later, I heard him moaning. I went to check on him. He was on his knees in the hallway. His forehead was pressed against the wall, his hands covered his eyes. It was a sad sight. I convinced him to get up. Once he was standing, he lifted his arms out to me. I went to him. I let him hold me and cry while I pat-ted his back. "Forgive me," he begged over and over again.

"Okay, Joe, but this is the last time," I heard myself say. I was in too much disarray to comprehend what was happening to me. I told myself he wouldn't be this remorseful, this upset, if he was a horrible guy. I told myself he was scared. But I was the one who was scared; scared to leave, scared to kick him out, and scared to admit the truth. Minimizing the truth was a method of coping and surviving.

His remorse was as ritualistic and cunning as his abuse. He wasn't re-ally sorry; he was simply giving me false hope. His apologizes were full of self pity and actual instructions on how I should behave so he didn't feel frightened or unloved. Because as long as he felt safe and loved, he wouldn't abuse me. He was making it my responsibility. I came to know his speeches off by heart: If I loved him as much as he loved me, he would forgive me no matter what I did. He loved me too much. I didn't love him enough, etc., etc., etc. I knew I was strong and I knew I was in-telligent, yet I didn't see he was strategically brainwashing me and break-ing my spirit. He performed his apologizes so convincingly he could have won an academy award. My mind was a maze of confusion.

For the next two weeks, he was kind, romantic and calm He took me shopping for new clothes one day. I tried on dresses, shirts and jeans. I modelled everything for him. He pretended he was the commentator of a fashion show, entertaining me and the sales assistant with his antics. It was the first time since the incident I felt relaxed. He declared I deserved to wear silk and bought me two silk blouses; one blue and one white. He also bought me a stylish black skirt. That evening we went out for dinner to my favourite restaurant. I wore the white silk blouse and my new skirt. He told me I looked like a model.

"I'm a lucky guy," he said during dinner.

"You're right, Joe. You're a lucky guy," I teased.

Chapter 11

A FEW DAYS AFTER the shopping spree and romantic dinner date, he struck again.

I was cooking dinner and had spaghetti sauce simmering in a pot when he got home from work. He went immediately to the sauce and sampled a spoonful. "It needs more garlic," he grunted.

"I used it all," I said. He clicked his tongue. My stomach tightened. I reached out and put my hand on his shoulder. "Can I have a kiss?" I asked in a childish voice that didn't sound like me. He gave me a quick kiss.

"I'm going to run over to the store and buy some garlic. I can't eat it like that," he said in a tone of disgust. I nodded as if I agreed with his critique, even though I didn't.

While he was gone, I cooked the pasta. My mind was grilling itself for suggestions on how I could lighten his mood. Optimistically, I thought he'd probably come back feeling more cheerful. I barely paid attention to how belittled I felt. Instead I focused on him and what I would do if he returned in the same mood. I decided I would ignore it; pretend I didn't notice. I'd thank him for going out and buying the garlic. I'd tell him I didn't know what I would do without him.

He returned wearing an expression of self pity. He slammed the garlic cloves down on the counter then poured himself a rum and coke. It was mostly rum. I could barely force a thank you out of my mouth. I wanted to tell him to fuck off. I wanted to tell him he was a rude bastard, an immature creep, but I didn't dare. I felt weak and pitiful. He ignored me and stormed out of the room. I added a tiny bit of garlic to the sauce knowing he would not notice how much or how little I put in. His ranting had nothing to do with the taste. It was just an excuse to get angry and belligerent. I drained the pasta, took the salad out of the fridge and set it on the counter. Then I called him to come and dish up. I poured myself a glass of red wine, leaned up against the counter and waited for him to join me in the kitchen. He took his time getting there, so I went ahead and dished a tiny portion onto my plate. I had lost my appetite. I was heading into the dining room when he came into the kitchen.

"What the fuck is this?" he yelled, holding up a tong full of pasta.

"What do you mean?" I asked as calmly as I could.

"You have enough pasta to feed an army. What's going on?" He glared at me suspiciously.

"I made too much pasta. Oh well," I said, looking at him. His dark, angry eyes shot fear into my heart. I told myself not to provoke him.

"You made a mess of dinner because you don't give a shit about me. If you were thinking about me the way I always think about you, you would have been trying to make a nice meal." He was beyond shouting, he was roaring. "When I cook for you, all I think about is pleasing you. Not you, Leah, you're too busy thinking about your band guys. I'm sick of this shit!" His breathing was heavy. He picked up the bowl of pasta and threw it in the garbage, then he grabbed the bowl holding the sauce and dumped it down the sink. It spattered across the counter top and over the edges. It looked like blood. It looked like a crime scene. I stood there frozen, frightened and alone. *No! Not again. Not again.* He grabbed me by the hair with one hand and walloped me across the face with the other. I felt the terrible sting and cried out. The room started spinning. I was being yanked into the living room. I was on the floor. He was sitting on my stomach. He was belting me across my face and head. He was pinning my arms with his knees. I was kicking my legs, lifting my hips, struggling to get him off me. He was calling me names; an ungrateful bitch, a fucking slut, a fucking cunt, a fucking whore.

Finally he climbed off me. I was sobbing. I crawled over to the couch and pulled myself onto it. He marched to the kitchen and returned with a fresh drink in his hand. I wished I had a drink. I wished I could disappear. I wished he would disappear. He sat on the chair and glared at me. I hoped he would soon go into his self-pitying stage; at least he would stop hitting me then. It didn't take long.

"Stop crying." he ordered "You have nothing to cry about. I'm the one who's hurt. How do you think I feel? I think about you all day. I can't wait until I get home to see you. But you, you selfish, fucking bitch don't give a shit about me. You can't even be bothered to cook me a decent meal." His words helped refuel his anger. I tried to talk. I tried to tell him he was wrong, but each time I tried to speak he yelled louder. "Shut up! Shut your ugly mouth!"

It went on for hours. He lectured me until he got worked up enough to beat me again. He told me I was ugly and stupid. "You're almost forty years old and you have nothing. You're a fucking loser, Leah. You don't know how to love, that's why you're divorced."

"You're divorced too," I managed to fling back.

He stiffened and gritted his teeth. "From a bitch just like you. I'm fucking sick of being screwed around by selfish women. You're going to change, Leah. I'm not going through another break up. You better fucking change if you know what's good for you."

I couldn't stand the thought of what was coming. I had to get out of there. I waited until he went to the bathroom then opened the door quietly and slipped out. The minute I was in the hallway I panicked. I was afraid to try running down the stairs in case he caught up with me. He might shove me down the stairs. I was afraid to knock on a neighbour's door. *What if they don't answer? What if they won't help me?* I ran down the hallway and hid in the laundry room. It was late, no one was doing laundry. I stood in the darkness, pressed against the wall. I prayed for help. Within minutes I heard someone walking heavily down the hallway. I knew it was him. Anguished tears poured from my eyes. *Please protect me, God.* The door swung open. I was tucked behind it. I held my breath. Suddenly his hand clutched my wrist and violently jerked me out into the hallway. He kept his grip firm as he silently led me back to the apartment. I told myself to scream at the top of my lungs, but I couldn't. I was frozen. As soon as we were back inside, he spun into a demonic rage.

"You can't ever leave me. You hear me? Get that through your head. I will fucking kill you. Look at me!" He held my face and dug his fingers in so hard I thought he was going to break my jaw. The pain was excruciating. "You know I'll do it. No matter where you go, I'll find you. I know people, Leah, and you know what I'm talking about. People who would do anything for me, people who can make you disappear without a trace. Don't ever walk out on me again. Remember, I know where to find your kids. I know how to hurt you, and I will. I'm sick of being a nice guy and getting shit on." His cruel eyes pierced through mine. He looked evil. I didn't doubt his threats.

As soon as he finished his tirade, he knocked me to the floor, put his hands around my throat and choked me. I couldn't breathe. I was frantic. I thought he was going to kill me. I tried to loosen his grip, but I was completely helpless. Finally he let go. He sneered down at me and spat in my face. Then he yanked me up off the floor by my hair. I cried out in pain. My nose and lip were bleeding and my scalp was burning. My spirit was completely shattered.

That night he enforced a new rule; I wasn't allowed to sit on his furniture. I had to sit on the floor and look up at him, look him in the eyes while he demeaned and threatened me. "You look at me when I'm talking to you or I'll knock your teeth out. You look away once and you'll be toothless. What would your band buddies think of you then?"

Like a frightened child, I obeyed. Thoughts swirled through my head as I sat there dehumanized and afraid to even blink. I wondered why the neighbours didn't phone the police. *They must hear him. Please someone phone the police, help me. Please protect me, God.* I felt I was coming undone, falling to pieces right there on the floor. It took every bit of strength I had just to hold myself together.

Finally, after several hours, he started to crash. He literally ran out of steam. He said he was going to bed and ordered me to do the same. It was awful to lie next to him in bed, but I was too exhausted to resist the opportunity to sleep. Sleep, the great escape. I slept until he woke me early the next morning. He was kneeling on the floor beside me, softly stoking my hair. I opened my eyes and instantly burst into uncontrollable sobs.

"Oh baby, I'm so sorry. I'm so sorry. I love you. I love you so much," he said softly and urgently. He rose up and sat next to me. He tried to hold my hand. I yanked it away from him. I couldn't talk, I was crying hysterically. I rolled on my side, away from him, and pulled the sheet over my face. He rubbed my back. "How could I have hurt you, Leah? I love you. I'm sorry Princess, my beautiful, sweet Leah."

"Leave me alone," I sobbed. His words of repentance sickened me, but at least I knew I was out of danger for the time being.

"I'll go make us coffee and we can talk," he said

"I don't want to talk to you."

"Calm down, Leah, we have to talk. We have to," he said sternly.

"I can't believe you're telling me to calm down after what you did," I hissed. I heard him sigh then leave the room. I got up and went to the bathroom. I avoided the mirror at first. I was scared to look. When I finally did scan my reflection, I was relieved to see that it wasn't as bad as I had expected. It broke my heart and crushed my spirit to feel a sense of gratitude because he hadn't beaten my face as badly as I had feared. My lip was swollen and my eyes were puffy. There was no sign of bruises around my eyes but my hands, which had taken most of the blows while shielding my face and head, were covered with blotches of yellow. I knew they would soon turn purple and blue.

My body hurt as I walked down the hall and into the living room. He had coffee made and poured. A cup was waiting for me.

"Am I allowed to sit on your furniture?" I asked sarcastically. I couldn't look at him but I felt his eyes on me.

"Yes, Leah, and I'm sorry about that. I was just so hurt that you ran out of here. Don't do that again. It pushed me over the edge. You don't know how much I love you. I wish you loved me as much as I love you," he whined. He was blaming me. I was too furious to speak.

We sat in silence for a few seconds then he broke down. I had never seen a man who could cry the way he did. His body shook and trembled with each agonizing sob. I watched him for a few minutes feeling a degree of satisfaction for his misery. Finally, after I couldn't stand watching his self-indulgent suffering any longer, I went to him. I sat on the arm of the chair and put my arm around him. He let out a wretched moan, and I patted his back. In a small way, comforting him made me feel less of a victim, but mostly it was an act of self-preservation. I knew I'd be punished if I ignored his pain.

He wrapped his arms around my waist and held on tight. He said he had never hit a woman before and he would never do it again. He said he loved me too much and he would die for me. He cried, his head pressed against my shoulder for comfort. He looked vulnerable.

Angrily, I reminded him, in detail, what he had done to me the night before. He whimpered his apology over and over again then excused himself. I heard him in the bathroom blowing his nose. I sat back down on the couch and tried to sort through my thoughts and tangled emotions. Part of me felt sorry for him. I was in a state of confusion. I felt love and hatred but never at the same time. I felt inferior and superior but never at the same time. I felt weak and strong but never at the same time. I felt ashamed *all* the time. He had hinted he would hurt my kids and my friends if I left him. I couldn't risk their safety. My fear was as confining as a prison. I was trapped.

One evening a few days after the violent episode, he came home from work early. He had two dozen roses, lavender-scented candles, bubble-bath and a bag full of seafood. He said he wanted to cook for me. First he helped me put the flowers into vases then he prepared the bathroom for me. He filled the tub with hot water and bubble-bath, lit the candles and put on soft music. As I soaked in the warm water and inhaled the calming aroma, I told myself everything was going to be okay. Only a minute part of me believed it, but I clung to that shard of belief. I dismissed the bruises on my body and the fear in my heart. I wanted to feel loved, safe and peaceful, but I also longed to feel free.

After I had soaked for quite a while, he knocked on the door then opened it. He came over and knelt beside the bath tub. He looked so innocent.

"You're the most beautiful woman I've ever met, Leah," he whispered as he gently massaged my back with a soapy cloth. He helped me out of the tub and hummed as he dried my back. "Hurry and get dressed, dinner is almost ready," he said as he patted my butt. I rushed into my bedroom and pulled on a snug fitting dress that looked like a long T-shirt. I didn't bother putting on a bra or panties. I wasn't sure whether I was placating him to avoid another scene or if I was still kidding myself I would enjoy making love with him. We ate a magnificent meal, drank a little wine then made love on the living room floor.

The next morning I felt I was a sick participant in a sick relationship. Shame was rapidly replacing my dignity and sense of self worth.

Chapter 12

ONE MORNING ABOUT two weeks later, I woke up early and crept out of the bedroom. Joe was sleeping soundly. For some reason, he wasn't going to work until noon. I made myself a cup of coffee then took it with me to my office. I was sorting through some paper work when the phone rang. I quickly answered it.

"Good morning, Leah," he greeted softly.

"Good morning, Terry," I replied.

"Sorry to call so early."

"That's okay, I'm surprised you're up; I thought all musicians slept until noon," I joked.

"I know. I don't think I've been up this early for years," he said with a laugh.

"To tell you the truth, I'm not usually up this early either, or at least not at work this early." It was a little after eight.

"I thought you probably got up with the birds, Leah."

"I had to get rid of my rooster, the neighbours were complaining."

He laughed then said, "The reason I'm calling is to tell you we had a problem at the club last night." I asked him what happened. "This drunken jerk stood in the middle of the dance floor yelling at us to get off the stage and calling us every name in the book. Finally, after this went on for a while, a bouncer came over to escort the guy out. The guy threw his beer glass and hit Tim in the head. Tim's okay, but it stunned the hell out of him." He spoke calmly. "We're pretty pissed off that something wasn't done sooner. I mean, this guy started harassing us the minute we got on stage. I kept looking over at the bouncer and he just stood there oblivious. Anyway what's his name, the manager?"

"Tony," I said, furious over what had happened.

"Yeah, Tony wasn't there so I thought maybe you should let him know what happened."

I assured him I would, then we talked for a few minutes longer. He asked me if I was coming out to see them this week. I wasn't planning on it, but I didn't tell him that. After hearing what happened I decided I had to go as a show of support. I told him I'd come out later in the week. He thanked me and said he looked forward to seeing me.

It was too early to try to get hold of Tony, so I made a note in my day timer to call him at ten. I heard Joe stirring in the other room. I shouted a good morning to him. He mumbled good morning back on his way to the bathroom. I typed up a few contracts while he showered. A little while later he came into my office.

"Why did you get out of bed so early?" he asked, looking at me with distrust.

"I was wide awake so I decided to get some work done," I explained patiently, even though I felt uneasy. "Did you have a good sleep?" I smiled, hoping to relax him.

"It scared me when I woke up and you weren't there." I felt my body stiffen. *Don't act nervous.*

"You were sleeping peacefully; I wasn't going to wake you to tell you I was getting up. That would have been rude." I kept the edge out of my voice, but I was feeling bitter at having to explain myself.

"I wouldn't have thought it was rude," he snapped. He turned and walked out of the room.

If he thinks I need his permission to get out of bed, he's nuts. I tried to focus my attention on work and ignore the knot tightening in my stomach. I decided a long, hot shower would distract and relax me.

"I'm having a shower," I yelled out to him on my way to the bathroom. He didn't respond.

I could hear the television blaring and wondered if he even heard me. I considered peeking in on him to make sure he didn't need the bathroom for a while but I couldn't be bothered, so I yelled a little louder, "Do you need the bathroom? I'm going to shower."

"I heard you the first time, go ahead." He sounded uninterested in what I was doing and that was a relief. My stomach muscles relaxed.

After I showered and dressed I went back into my office. He was sitting at my desk with a grim look on his face. He pointed to a chair and told me to sit down. I sat down, folded my arms, and nervously waited to hear what was on his mind. He reached down towards the floor behind the desk and pulled up a recording devise. He set in on the desk. I was baffled. I'd never seen the recorder before. I could see there was tape in it. *Is he going to play a song for me?* He pressed the play button and I heard Terry's voice first, then mine. He had recorded our conversation. I couldn't believe it. I was furious, but I was also terrified. I asked him as calmly as I could why he had recorded my conversation.

"I knew I couldn't trust you, and here's the proof!" He turned the volume up then yelled over it. "You fucking slut, flirting with that prick. The only reason you were talking about sleeping in and shit is because you wanted him to think about you in bed."

He called me several more of his favourite degrading names and then accused me of planning to go out and meet Terry behind his back. He snarled and growled like a vicious animal. I sat there full of dread, wishing I hadn't talked to Terry.

With a smirk on his face, he picked up a container full of paperclips and threw it to the floor. About a hundred of the tiny clips flew out and covered the carpet. He ordered me to get down and pick them up. I was too scared to defend my conversation with Terry, but I had to defend some little bit of my honour. "No, I'm not picking them up," I snapped. He looked at me disdainfully, then in one quick motion he was out of his chair and behind mine. He grabbed the back of my chair and tipped it forward so I lost my balance and fell forward onto the floor. I was on my hands and knees. When I tried to get up he forced my head to the floor. I struggled. He pressed my head down harder. I could feel the carpet burning my face. I collapsed.

He released the pressure on my head then once again ordered me to pick up the paper clips. Like a slave, I obeyed. Like a slave owner, he supervised while I crawled around the floor doing his bidding. I tried not to see myself as I must have looked. I tried not be eaten alive by my humiliation. *It's okay; you're doing what you have to do.*

I picked up most of the paperclips. He dumped them again. I picked them up again. We spent the whole day in the tiny office. He played the tape over and over again, each time fuelling his rage into a violent tantrum. He smacked me in the face repeatedly. He yanked me around by my hair, yelling at me, "You dye your hair blond to get attention from men. You need to fucking cut it. It's too long, you just want to be noticed, you fucking whore, fucking little slut." He twisted my arm behind my back and demanded to know how many times I had had sex with Terry. I told him I had never had sex with Terry. He made me swear to that on the lives of my children.

Several times throughout the long, terrifying day my phone rang. He wouldn't let me answer it. Sometimes he answered; sometimes he let the answering machine get it. When he did answer, he told the caller I was out for the day then asked who was calling and what it was regarding. I was embarrassed by his curtness. I felt so helpless and hopeless sitting there with no rights. I was more afraid of what might happen than of what was happening now. What if Terry phoned back? What would Joe say to him? I could imagine him interrogating Terry. I could imagine Terry telling him to fuck off and not wanting anything to do with either one of us ever again. I wanted to phone Tony as I had promised. What excuse was I going to give Terry? My boyfriend held me hostage in my office all day. He beat me up several times. He forced me to sit on a chair facing him while he called me insulting names. At one point I had to go to the bathroom. He wouldn't let me leave the room unless I got down on my knees and asked for his permission. I refused. He retaliated. So I did it; I got down on my knees in front of him and asked him for permission to leave the office and go to the bathroom. Once in the bathroom I told myself it was okay because at least I had a few minutes to myself, away from him. So anyway, Terry, that's why I couldn't phone Tony. Sorry.

Around six in the evening he decided he was hungry, so he ordered a pizza. I was instructed to get out of the office. He said he wanted to phone Dominique. I went into the living room and guided my sore, tired body into the soft chair. I lit a cigarette and watched the smoke as I exhaled, wishing I could float away with it. I could hear him on the phone. He was speaking Italian, the way he always did when he phoned

Dominique, in a loud and angry voice. I wanted a drink. I went into the kitchen and poured myself a glass of wine. I saw the rum on the table; it was almost empty. He had drunk several shots throughout the afternoon. By the time he was off the phone I was sitting in the living room drinking my second glass of wine. It wasn't calming me the way I hoped.

"I told Dominique what you did. He's so fucking mad he's going to jump on a plane and come out here to pay you a visit. You're lucky, Leah. Your fucking lucky I talked him out of it. You don't know how lucky you are. He wants to take you away for a while, teach you how to behave like a proper lady. No one would find you, Leah. You're kids might never see you again. They'll think you abandoned them. Is that what you want?" He was standing in the middle of the room waving his hands in the air with every stupid word he said.

I shook my head. I didn't want to talk. I didn't want to take the chance of saying something that would rile him more. He mumbled to himself as he made his way to the kitchen. He was almost out of rum and announced he was going to the liquor store. He reminded me the pizza would soon be here. I quickly thanked God that he was going to leave for a little while. I peeked outside and watched his car pull out away. Then I scurried down the hall into the office. The taping devise was sitting on the desk, unplugged. I checked my phone for any extra cords. I looked up Tony's phone number, but before I dialed it I hit redial. I wanted to write Dominique's number down, hide it somewhere, maybe give it to someone in case I did suddenly disappear. I stared at the screen where the last number called appeared — it was Joe's parent's phone number.

The truth exploded in my brain; Dominique was fictitious! My knees went weak, I sat down. I should have known. He made numerous calls to Dominique yet there had been no long-distance calls to Seattle on my phone bill. When I mentioned it to him he said Dominique had a system with the phone company. I didn't bother to ask him what that meant because I didn't care.

I pushed this stunning revelation out of my mind long enough to phone Tony and tell him about the band's experience. He was thoughtful and assured me his bouncer would get a talking to. He also said he was working the rest of the week and no one would be harassing the band. I felt relieved and less defeated, at least for a while.

The pizza came before Joe got home. I set it on the kitchen counter and went into the living room. I felt as though I was sitting in a dark room, even though the sun was glaring through the window. Now that I could focus on my discovery that Joe had not been calling Dominique, I didn't even ponder any other explanation other than that he was fictitious. I knew with every inch of my being it was true. I was relieved in one way, but in another way I was more scared than ever; it meant that Joe was even crazier than I thought.

I heard his key in the door. *I've got to get as far away from this lunatic as possible.* I sat numb and stiff. He came in quietly. I heard him in the kitchen taking dishes out of the cupboard, opening the fridge, closing the fridge. Soon he strode into the living room with a plate of pizza in one hand and a glass of wine in the other. He placed both on the end table beside me.

I couldn't contain it. I had to say something. I wanted him to know I knew. I wanted to shame him. He went back into the kitchen and returned with his own plate of pizza and a drink. I waited until he sat down.

"Dominique phoned while you were gone," I said in a serious tone. He looked so bewildered I almost started laughing.

"You're lying," he snapped.

"He wants you to call him right away."

"He didn't phone. He doesn't phone anyone," he stuttered, unable to hide his discomfort.

"Maybe it's an emergency, Joe. If you don't believe me call him and ask," I said, feeling surprised and proud of my boldness.

His face reddened. I was suddenly too frightened to continue. Just then the phone rang. Joe jumped up and answered it. It was his dad. Joe talked to him in Italian. I wondered if the conversation he had pretended to have with Dominique was on his parent's answering machine. They would have been at work at the time. I had no idea what Joe was saying. I wondered if his parents knew how crazy he was or if they lived in denial. I wondered whether they would help. I decided they'd probably be too afraid.

He hung up the phone and instantly began to rant about parents, claiming he wished they had left him with his aunt. "What kind of parents would give their child away for two years?" He looked at me for confirmation that I had heard him. I didn't say anything. He wanted me to feel sorry for him, and in a way I did. I felt sorry for him because he was too chicken to be normal.

His childhood sob story eventually evolved into a tearful apology. He said he wasn't sorry for taping my calls but he was sorry for hitting me and calling me names. Later he showed me how he had set up the recorder in the closet of the office and ran the cord along the bottom of the baseboard and into my phone jack. He said as soon as I picked up the phone it began recording. He told me he bought it a long time ago to record threatening phone calls his ex-wife was making to him after he left her. I didn't believe him. I asked him why he was taping me. He said he did it because I'd been acting nervous and guilty the last few days; he was suspicious. *I'm a nervous wreck because of you, you creep.*

"I just needed to make sure you're not cheating on me. I don't want to get hurt," he said, sounding like a broken record.

"I'm the one getting hurt," I said, unable to stop the tears — tears that tried to wash away the pain from inside. I hated my dreadful life.

"I know. I shouldn't have reacted like that. I love you so much that when I heard you talking to Terry I lost it. I wish you'd taped my phone calls, at least I'd know you cared." He spoke his nonsense in a calm, almost soothing voice. He believed he was making sense. I wanted to say I'd be happy to tape his phone calls with Dominique, but I didn't. I wanted peace more than retaliation.

Joe never mentioned Dominique again after that day, and neither did I. I felt I had achieved a small victory by busting him in his lie but that didn't remove my constant fear. I knew he had invented Dominique to intimidate and control me. I wondered what else he had lied about. I was past the point of being shocked by his deceit. I was shocked only by the realization that he was far more dangerous than I had feared. Gone was my vision of a violently passionate, jealous, brutal man. I realized he was psychotic.

Chapter 13

NOTHING WAS CLEAR to me except that if I left him I would suffer consequences much worse than the consequences of staying. I was thoroughly indoctrinated to believe there was no escaping him. I was overwhelmed. I prayed things would get better.

Things didn't get better; they got worse. October and November were a living nightmare. Something I did or said would provoke him into a jealous tantrum. He'd begin his ritualistic abuse by forcing me to sit on the floor and look at him while he conducted a long lecture on what I did wrong and what I should have done. I was a prisoner with no rights. I tried not to drown in my own humiliation. I tried to float above it. When I felt myself sinking I'd think of something to hang on to. I knew the one thing he couldn't control were my thoughts. I could think freely. I'd think about how ludicrous he sounded and looked, how crazy he was, what an asshole he was. I'd sooth myself with a promise that I would someday, somehow, be free from him, but he would never be free — he would always be stuck with himself.

I prayed almost constantly during those days. I prayed for help, but eventually I didn't feel worthy of asking God for help so I began to pray in gratitude. I'd thank God for each day there were no violent episodes. When there was an episode, I'd thank God when it ended. I'd thank God for my children and ask that He protect them from the truth. I was positive my family and friends would never understand how dangerous he was. They wouldn't understand why I couldn't leave. They'd be disappointed in me, they'd lose respect for me, be completely disgusted with me. I thought they would think those things because I thought them about myself. Whatever self-esteem I'd had before I met Joe was disappearing along with my self-respect. Sometimes I would lie in bed and visualize saving my own soul; hiding it somewhere safe where it could stay whole.

I spent hours and hours trying to devise a plan to escape and be safe. That was my dilemma: leaving would have been easy, but leaving and living in safety seemed impossible. I witnessed his vicious capabilities first hand, and I believed without a shred of doubt that he would torture and kill me if I left him. He said I would suffer for hurting him. He said he would hurt my kids and I'd know it was my fault and they would know it was my fault too. He swore if I left him he'd find me. He said he'd kidnap me then take me deep into a forest and chain me up. He said no one would find me. He looked excited whenever he described his sick fantasies of destroying me. He said he'd kill me before he'd see me with another man. "That's true love," he'd claim.

Somehow I functioned. I worked hard at my job and I talked to my kids on a regular basis. It seemed like a blessing that they were busy with their own lives and not concerned that we weren't spending a lot of time together. I phoned Carrie almost every day. Since we were both self employed and working from our homes, we could indulge in long conversations, which we called our coffee breaks. We'd talk about our kids, our jobs, and politics. We'd discuss issues, especially women's issues, share our opinions on a current news story or reminisce about some of our past adventures together. Those conversations were my life line, my connection to a world outside my prison. I never talked about Joe unless she brought him up. I'd tell her he was fine and that everything was going well between us. I'd tell her something nice about him, something he did for me or bought for me. Whenever she suggested we get together I would put her off with an excuse. Usually I told her I was expecting an important call or I had a meeting. She always understood. I could only imagine her horror if I told her the truth: *I'm not allowed anywhere without Joe. If he phoned and I wasn't here I would suffer a severe punishment.* It sounded ridiculous and pathetic. It was ridiculous and pathetic.

Chapter 14

ONE MONDAY NEAR the end of November, Carrie phoned and suggested we have a girl's night out later in the week. My heart sank.

"This week is crazy, we've got something going on every night, but, yes, we will do that soon. I'd love it," I said, faking my enthusiasm and hating myself for lying to my best friend.

"Can you get away for lunch tomorrow?"

"Sure," I said while trying to think up the excuse I would use later to cancel.

"I'll call you in the morning."

We said good bye and I hung up. I sat for a few minutes picturing her pretty face and kind smile. A lump rose in my throat; I furiously fought back tears. I missed seeing her, I missed living my life. I was lonely and isolated. The only time I had seen her in the past couple of months was one Sunday Joe and I went to their place for coffee. I felt so uncomfortable; I didn't dare look Ken in the eyes when he talked. I faked a headache about forty-five minutes after we arrived.

I could hear Joe in the kitchen and I knew he was making dinner. He had come home at noon and said he was taking the afternoon off. At one point I heard him whistling and it irritated me because it felt as though he was bragging about his freedom to do whatever he wanted. I found myself imagining him suddenly dropping dead of a heart attack.

Suddenly he was in the doorway, smiling. He announced dinner would be ready in an hour and wondered if I wanted to take a break and have a cocktail with him. I put on an artificial smile and told him I'd join him in a few minutes. I wanted to have a good night. I wanted him to go to work the next day so I could sneak out and meet Carrie for lunch. I took a minute to silently thank God for Carrie's friendship.

The table was set and I could smell roast beef cooking. He was busy peeling potatoes over the kitchen sink. He looked so normal and I thought how great it would be if he was. I was surprised at how good my appetite was by the time we sat down to eat. I complimented him on the meal. He smiled, then for no apparent reason he began to weep. I wanted to scream at him to shut up. I was fed up with him acting like he was the victim.

"Why are you crying?' I asked, trying to sound as though I actually cared.

"I love you so much sweet pea. I want to make you happy all the time," he whimpered.

"You made a nice meal; relax and enjoy it," I said, hearing a motherly tone in my voice. He smiled and instantly shifted into a good mood.

After dinner he wanted to go shopping to buy me a winter jacket. I didn't want to go shopping; going anywhere in public with him was dangerous. He had invented this preposterous rule that I couldn't look at anyone, male or female, for more than three seconds. According to him more than three seconds of eye contact meant I was sending signals; sexual signals. If a guy looked at me, it was my fault. He claimed a man only looks at a woman if she's sending signals. He said he had read it in a psychology book. It was a no-win situation for me. I was trying to think of a way out of it when suddenly a loud gust of wind shook the window pane. We looked at each other then rushed to the window. The wind was howling and blowing a huge cloud of dust across the parking lot.

"I don't want to go out there," I said.

"I don't either," he said. "Maybe we're going to get a snow storm."

"Maybe," I said. My gratitude for the strong winds quickly turned into despair as I considered being cooped up with him all winter. "I hope not," I said.

He put his arm around me and guided me over to the couch. He told me to sit and relax while he tidied up. I offered to help but he insisted on working alone. Before long he came back and sat down on the edge of the chair across from me.

"Do you stand and look out the window when you're here alone?" he asked me suspiciously.

"No."

"Are you sure?"

"I'm positive," I said. It was obvious he had a concern about me looking out the window. *What an idiot.*

"Good, because you never know, someone might be watching you. There are a lot of creeps out there, Leah. Someone could see you standing in the window, figure out which apartment you live in, break in and rape you or something."

I agreed with him, even though I was thinking it takes one to know one. Satisfied, he returned to the kitchen and finished cleaning up. I reminded myself of Carrie's invitation to meet for lunch and I started wishing we would get a snow storm. She probably wouldn't want to go out if the weather was crappy. On the other hand, I really wanted to see her. I wanted to do something normal. I started thinking of ways I could pull it off. I figured I could stop at the fish market and buy some prawns and scallops, then if Joe tried to call me or came home, I'd say I went out to shop so I could make him a seafood dinner. I could stop at the bakery and the wine store as well to cover up the time. I could tell Carrie I was expecting an important business call and had only an hour for lunch. I could suggest we go to Ruby's, a nice restaurant just down the street from the fish market. My biggest worry with the plan was that Joe would drive by and see my car. He'd definitely stop and come in. He'd embarrass the hell out of me. With that thought, my mind swiftly jumped back to wishing for a snow storm. I could feel my shoulders slump.

Later that night I lay in bed listening to the wind. It had died down to a mournful sounding breeze. Joe was sound asleep. I hated being in bed with him, but I was grateful for his lack of interest in sex lately. When he did want to have sex I didn't refuse; I didn't dare reject him in any way. When he didn't want sex, I thanked God.

I was already wide awake when his alarm clock rang in the morning. I got up and made a pot of coffee. He showered, shaved, got dressed then joined me at the table. I asked him if he wanted something to eat. As usual, he said he didn't. I wondered if he even remembered the time he punished me for not making him breakfast. We sat in silence for a few minutes. I couldn't help noticing how attractive he looked in his black shirt and black pants. I told him he looked nice. He smiled brightly and thanked me. *You can't judge a book by its cover.*

"What are you doing today?" he asked, as if I could say whatever I wanted and he'd be fine with it.

"Working," I said bluntly.

"Maybe I'll come and get you for lunch; it depends on my work load. I wish my office wasn't so far away, it'd be nice to come home for lunch every day," he said looking into my eyes for a response.

"I was thinking the same thing," I lied. I could feel butterflies swarming in my stomach. *Does he suspect something?* He had never taken me out for lunch on a work day since he'd moved in. He had never even mentioned it. I concentrated on hiding my nervousness. I put love in my eyes and looked deeply into his. "I hope you can get away at lunch time. That would be fun. Let me know so I can be ready when you get here, or maybe I could meet you somewhere in the middle." I was so believable I amazed myself. I didn't feel guilty about lying to him because it was vital to my safety and survival.

He kissed and hugged me. He told me he loved me with all his heart. As soon as he left I took a deep breath and thanked God that he had gone.

I looked outside, the sky was clear, the wind had calmed. I knew I couldn't go out with Carrie. It was too risky. I spent my time in the shower trying to think up a decent excuse to give her. Lying to Joe was one thing, but lying to everyone else was stripping my self-respect away and replacing it with shame. I had no safe place to release the rage and bitterness building inside me. I felt it ripping me apart. I got out of the shower, lay down on my bed and cried. I cried long and loud. I cried until I was tired of crying.

I had just sat down at my desk when Carrie phoned. I had decided to tell her I had forgotten that I made a lunch date with Joe. It was partially true. To my surprise, she began the conversation with an apology.

"I'm sorry, Leah, but I'm going to have to cancel our lunch. I've got two sick little girls home from school today."

"Awe, that's too bad. Do they have the flu?" I inquired feeling ashamed for being so relieved.

"Yeah, they were both up during the night puking their little guts out."

"Poor kids," I said.

"Maybe we can go out for lunch next week."

"That sounds good," I said. *I'll try Carrie, I'll try.*

Joe called me a while later. He said he would pick me up right at noon. I asked him if he was sure he didn't want me to meet him somewhere closer to his work. He told me he didn't want me to drive across town. "I'd rather pick you up and take you home. That way I know you're safe. You know how I worry about you."

"I'd like to go to the fish market and buy some seafood for supper, so why don't we go to Ruby's. I can meet you there then go shopping after. I also want to go to the bakery and wine store." Then, for safety's sake I added, "Unless you have time to come shopping with me."

"I'll make time. I don't have to be back here until two," he said abruptly.

"That sounds good. See you at noon," I said, faking happiness.

"I love you."

"I love you too," I said dutifully. I hung up the phone and slumped back in my chair. I hated my life. I hated him. I hated me. I didn't want to have lunch with him. I wanted to make my own choice, that's what I truly wanted.

The phone rang. I pulled myself together and answered it. Guy Cool's cheerful voice greeted me. "Good morning, lovely Leah."

I had checked my phone earlier to make sure I wasn't being taped, but I was still unnerved by Guy's greeting. "How are you, Guy?" I replied in my professional phone voice.

"Excellent. It's nice to have a few days off."

"I bet. You guys have been working hard. I'm getting really good feedback on the band, you're doing a great job."

"You're doing a great job too. We appreciate the gigs and the money you're getting us," he said humbly. Then he asked if he could drop by later and drop off my commission. I tensed. If Joe walked in and Guy was here, it would be a disaster. My other clients mailed my commissions to me. I actually felt a little annoyed he didn't do the same. Under other circumstances I would have been extremely grateful he was willing to come over and pay me.

"I'm heading out in a few minutes and I'm not sure what time I'll be home. You can mail me a cheque or money order," I said breezily.

"No, I'll drop it off. I can come by tomorrow, I'd like to see you." I told him that would be fine, even though I wasn't sure it would be.

I was ready and waiting when Joe picked me up. On our way to the restaurant he was chatty and obviously in a good mood. I relaxed a little. The restaurant was busy and the service was slow. He called our waitress over twice to ask how much longer our meal would be. The second time he was quite rude. She looked upset and I felt sorry for her.

"It's not her fault," I said after she walked away.

"Are you taking her side?"

"No." *What a jerk.*

A short time later I saw the waitress approaching with our meals. Behind her I saw Guy Cool and a couple of the guys in his band. They were being led to a table across from ours. Oh shit! I turned my eyes away quickly. I knew it was only a matter of time before Guy noticed me. I braced myself. As if following instructions from another source, I stretched my leg under the table and rubbed Joe's ankle with my foot. He looked over at me and smiled slightly. I smiled lovingly back at him. He appeared consoled.

Just minutes later I heard Guy call my name. Joe turned around so quickly I was surprised he didn't get whiplash. I looked over at Guy with an expression of surprise. They all smiled and waved at me. I waved back.

"Who's that?" Joe demanded, his eyes flashing anger and suspicion.

I told him. I tried to have a conversation with him during lunch but he simply gave blunt answers. He did not make eye contact. He ate fast; I had a hard time eating at all. I forced down what I could then pushed my plate away claiming I was full.

As soon as we stood up to go, he grabbed my hand and held it tightly while leading me out of the restaurant. I glanced over at Guy and gave him a quick little wave. He nodded but I thought he looked offended. I felt terrible. I was his agent and I didn't even stop and talk to him. I could barely contain the rage inside me from exploding.

We didn't do any shopping after lunch. He drove straight back to the apartment. It was only a few blocks but it felt like miles. He asked me if I knew Guy was going to be there. I told him I didn't.

"I just think it's pretty weird. You didn't want me to pick you up. Maybe the reason you wanted to meet me near my office was so you could sneak back to Ruby's to meet Guy. I would have been all the way across town at my office so you wouldn't have to worry about me catching you with another guy."

"It was me who suggested we go to Ruby's," I reminded him.

"After I said I would pick you up," he shouted.

"You're accusing me of something I didn't do or plan on doing or ever have done," I said as calmly as I could, hoping he'd realize how irrational he was being. He didn't answer. He pulled up in front of the building. I felt a deep sense of relief he was dropping me off instead of coming in. I thanked him for lunch then went to kiss him. He turned away. I got out of the car. He skidded off dramatically.

I carried my dark, heavy feeling up the stairs. I reminded myself to simply be grateful he went back to work. I took my shoes off then hung my jacket in the closet. I went into the bathroom and started brushing my teeth. I didn't hear him come in. I didn't hear him come down the hallway. Suddenly there he was, standing behind me. I jumped and gasped when I saw his reflection in the mirror. He came up behind me and pressed his hand tightly over my mouth. I felt my body almost collapse. He ordered me to calm down before removing his hand.

"You scared me," I explained. Next thing I knew he was pulling me down the hallway into the living room, where he pushed me onto the floor. *No, please don't let this be happening.* He sat on my stomach and pounded my face with the back of his hand. He bellowed over and over again, "You fucking, lying, whore. You fucking slut."

Eventually he climbed off me. I tried to get up. My ears were ringing and my head felt light and dizzy. I had difficulty getting my balance. He told me I looked like a mental case then grabbed me by my hair and swung me across the room. I hit the wall. He charged towards me, pressed his arm across my neck and pinned me against the wall. I cried and begged him to stop. He pushed my head down towards the floor then brought his knee up into my stomach. I cried out in agony. My legs collapsed. He let me fall to the floor. I was curled up in a foetal position, my hands tightly folded over my tender stomach. He stood looking down at me for a few seconds then began kicking my legs and back. I tried to crawl away. He stomped on my back. I lay there enduring the pain until he stopped kicking me. *Just get through it,* just get through it. He pulled me up and ordered me to make him a drink. I made myself a drink too and gulped it down.

I heard him on the phone cancelling his afternoon meeting. I wanted to scream at the top of my lungs. My legs felt so weak and wobbly I wasn't sure they would carry me into the other room. He was sitting in his favourite chair glaring at me while I brought his drink to him.

"I hope you're happy," he snapped. "I had to cancel my meeting because I can't trust you. I can't go to work because you're a fucking liar and a fucking slut."

I sat down and pretended to listen to his long, rambling lecture. I wished I could video tape him so he could see, with his own eyes, a psycho in action. He went on and on for a couple of hours. I heard him yelling things like, stupid bitch, ugly bitch, and dumb bitch. I pretended, even to myself, his cruel words didn't hurt me.

The day dragged on. I heard my phone ring several times. He wouldn't allow me to answer.

After each call, he went and checked the answering machine. I sat with knots in my stomach, terrified one of the messages would send him back into a violent rage. I didn't feel a part of anything outside my small, dark world of abuse. I felt alone.

Joe drank so much throughout the afternoon that he passed out early in the evening. He had disappeared into the bedroom so I went to check on him. He was sprawled out across the bed, snoring. I silently thanked God then went out to the living room and poured myself a drink. I sank onto the couch, lit a cigarette and inhaled deeply.

I thought about other women who were in my situation. I wanted to reach out to them and tell them I understood their pain. I thought about children who endured abuse and it tore at my heart. I wanted to help all those women and children, but I couldn't even help myself. I didn't know how. I had convinced myself I couldn't go to a women's shelter because he'd go after my kids. I was certain I would have to leave town and take Chad and Myla with me. I wondered how I would explain to them that they had to give up their lives here because of my bad choice in a boyfriend. He was my problem not theirs. I had to solve this on my own. I couldn't involve my innocent kids or friends.

The following day he woke up well before his alarm clock rang. I pretended I was sleeping when he whispered my name. Of course, he didn't give up. "Sorry to wake you," he said. I didn't say anything. He gathered me into his arms and held me so tight I coughed. "I'm sorry baby, I got carried away yesterday. I'm so sorry. I love you so much."

All I wanted was for him to go to work. I knew I had to make him feel secure enough to do that. "I love you too, Joe," I whispered. "You have to trust me. I deserve to be trusted."

"You're right. You do deserve to be trusted. I promise I'll try harder. You have my word on that, Leah. I love you sweet pea. I'm so lucky to have you and I never want to lose you. I couldn't take it." He rocked me back and forth in his arms while he talked. *Please go to work. Please go to work. Please go to work.* After more apologies and his routine of begging for forgiveness, he finally left, but not before asking me to promise I would never leave him. I did.

I could barely move as a result of his abuse. I treated my aching body to a hot bath. While soaking I examined my legs and arms. I knew they would soon be covered in bruises and I began to sob in pain. I cried all morning. I tried to return my missed phone calls from the day before but every time I picked up the phone I broke down again. Finally I went and lay down on my bed and cried until I was out of steam. Then I began to calm down. It had been so long since I'd felt calm. I clung to the feeling. I forced myself to get back to work. Before long, I was making calls and sealing deals. Work was my therapy; it was mine, it was normal.

Early in the afternoon Guy phoned to say he was on his way over with my commission. He asked me if I had time for a coffee. I told him I wish I did but that I took too long a lunch and had to cram the rest of the afternoon. I hung up and ran to the bathroom to inspect my appearance. My eyes were puffy from crying. I swept a coat of mascara over my lashes, lightly brushed over my cheeks with blush and pulled my hair up into a pony tail. I closed the curtains in my office to block out the natural light. Just then the phone rang. It was Joe calling to tell me he loved me. I was relieved he called before Guy arrived.

I had no sooner hung up when the buzzer rang. I let Guy in. I had no idea Terry was with him until I opened my door. He gave me a big smile then walked over and hugged me. I hugged him back. I felt safe in his arms; a feeling I barely recalled.

"Should I leave you two alone?" Guy teased.

"Yeah, give us a couple hours," Terry joked. We all laughed as he released me. I wanted to go back into his arms. I wanted to cry on his shoulder.

We went into my office and I gave Guy a few contracts to sign. While he was busy with that, Terry and I talked. "I took a job driving truck," he informed me, "I start next week."

"Good for you. Do you still want to work with the band on weekends?" I asked, aware I was avoiding eye contact with him and hoping he didn't notice I was behaving like an abused woman.

"We're thinking about packing it in, Leah. We're burned out, sick of the bar scene," he said sounding apologetic. "Of course we'll play the dates you have booked."

"I'll sure miss working with you," I said sadly. "I mean, I understand though."

"I don't want to lose touch with you, Leah. Besides, once I'm no longer a client we can go on a date," he said flashing a mischievous grin. I must have looked a little nervous because he quickly added, "I'm just kidding. I know you have a boyfriend."

"I don't think he's kidding," Guy commented, looking at me with a sly smirk and a raised eyebrow. I felt myself blush. The phone rang. *Please don't be Joe.* It was Carrie. I told her I'd call her back. Terry and Guy prepared to leave, but before going out the door Terry turned to me and said he hoped I'd come out and see the band for their last performance. I promised I would be there, and I meant it.

I had a hard time getting him out of my head the rest of the afternoon. I knew he respected me and considered me a good friend. I knew he cared about me. I wondered if he would feel the same way if he knew I lived with a man who beat me.

I felt nervous when it got close to the time Joe would be home from work. I was afraid he would find some evidence that Guy and Terry had been here. I had hidden Guy's cheque in my filing cabinet. When he first moved in, Joe had persuaded me to close my bank account and open a joint account with him at a different bank. He controlled all the money. Every time we received a statement he went over it thoroughly. He took money out whenever he wanted to, never accounting for any of it. That day, I decided I would use the money from Guy to re-open my old account. I just had to figure out where to have my statements sent in case one came on a day he checked the mail. I knew Myla wouldn't mind if I had them sent to her. I could simply tell her a woman should always have a little money put away, just in case.

He arrived home with a bouquet of flowers and a box of chocolates. I pretended I was grateful for his gifts, but I was angry. I was angry he thought they made up for his abuse. I was mostly angry that I wasn't allowed to show my anger. He hugged and kissed me passionately without seeming to notice I cringed at his touch.

"Get changed into something pretty because I'm taking you out for dinner," he announced eagerly.

"I made Shepherd's pie. It's in the oven."

"We can finish cooking it and then eat it tomorrow. I made reservations at La Gare. It's a new French restaurant that just opened a couple of weeks ago. I read a review in the newspaper, it was an excellent review. I made reservations for seven o'clock." He looked and sounded extremely pompous.

I resigned myself to going out. I applied my make up slowly; I still had to take pride in my appearance. I put on the silk shirt he had bought me and my black slacks. He came into the room and said I looked beautiful. I smiled and thanked him.

The restaurant was very classy and the food was amazing. I couldn't get enough of the freshly-baked bread. The smell and taste reminded me of my mom's homemade buns. It was as though I could feel her comforting me. I allowed myself to enjoy a couple of hours of peace and normalcy. Joe was charming and attentive. I felt giddy from the wine and told him I wished he could always be like this. He swore to me he could and he would. I didn't believe him but I still wished it was true.

Chapter 15

A MONTH WENT BY without him physically abusing me. It was a confusing time. We had Sunday dinners with Myla and Chad, and we visited his parents several times. On one of those visits his mom told me about her experience coming to Canada. She and I were sitting at the kitchen table, and Joe and his dad were in the other room. She said Joe was two years old when they left Italy. Joe's dad had come over earlier with his parents and younger sister. She talked about how hard it was to leave her family. She showed me pictures of Joe when he was a baby and pictures of him as a toddler with his younger brothers. One picture was taken on his third birthday. All of a sudden I got a very creepy feeling. I asked her if they had any relatives in the United States. She told me they didn't; she said they had never been there. *There is no Aunt Maria, just as there's no Dominique. What a freak!*

I felt icy chills run through my body. I shivered and pulled my jacket up around my shoulders. She asked if I was cold. I said I was and she offered to get me a sweater. I told her I was fine, but I really wanted to tell her that her son was a psychopath. *How could she not know?* I don't remember what we talked about after that. I felt detached and frighteningly informed.

On the way home I told Joe a little about my conversation with his mom. I told him about her showing me pictures of him when he was little. It didn't click at all until I said I was surprised to see the pictures because I thought he had lived with his aunt when he was that age. His face turned to stone. "You didn't say anything about my aunt to my mom, did you?" he asked frantically.

"No, I just asked her if you guys had any relatives living in the states. She said no." I said with deliberate calmness. I knew I was taking a risk, but I wanted him to know that I knew. I was appalled he had wanted me to believe his parents had abandoned him. He was heartless. He never mentioned Aunt Maria again.

He didn't hit me during that time span, but he was still in control. I walked on eggshells. I censored everything I said before I said it. I was living in constant fear and I was wearing out. When he was in a good mood, I soaked it in. I craved feeling safe and took whatever morsels of that feeling I could get. When he was affectionate, I responded because I needed to feel normal. I hated having sex with him though, it repulsed me. It was just another thing I had no choice about.

One evening when we were watching a program on the television, he suddenly turned it off. He got up from his chair, came over to the couch and sat down beside me. He gently took hold of my hand and kissed it. Then he told me about a movie he had seen before he met me. He said it was about a couple who split up because the husband was a member of the mob, and when the wife found out she left him. He said they still loved each other but she couldn't live that life style. Eventually she met someone else and asked her husband for a divorce. I listened closely as he continued telling me the story. He said the husband couldn't stand the thought of his wife being with someone else so he went to see her one night and shot her.

"He loved her too much to let her go. That's true love, Leah," he said while studying my eyes for hints of something; fear I figured. He asked me if I had seen the movie. I told him I hadn't. He said he couldn't remember the name of it but he remembered that Jaclyn Smith was in. I wanted to debate his conclusion about the movie but an inner voice warned me not to say anything. I got up quickly and went to the bathroom. I sat on the edge of the tub feeling doomed. I tried to calm myself with promises I would be okay. I reminded myself it was just a movie; a movie he'd never mentioned before. He had probably just forgotten about it until now, and he would probably forget about it again. I didn't sleep a wink that night.

Chapter 16

I T WAS THE middle of December and I was dreading Christmas. My family and I had been planning it all year. We rented accommodations at a lodge in the mountains. It was to be the first Christmas in a few years that my mom, step father, siblings, nieces and nephews would be together. We were pretty spread out geographically, so getting everyone together had become a rare and special treat. Myla and Chad were really excited and I pretended to share their feelings. But I was terrified. I was terrified he would do something to prevent me from going. I was just as terrified of facing my family. I felt like a complete fraud.

Myla and I went Christmas shopping. It was the first time I'd been anywhere outside the apartment without Joe since he'd moved in. I was expecting him to insist on coming with us, but he didn't.

We spent the whole day at the mall. I bought Joe a black leather jacket. I resented buying him anything, never mind such an expensive gift, but I was sure it would please him. And if he was happy, I would be safe. He had spent days shopping and putting beautifully wrapped presents under the tree. They were all for me. It made me incredibly uneasy because I knew whatever I bought him wouldn't compare to what he bought me and he would, at some point, use that against me.

When I got home from the mall he greeted me at the door and immediately unloaded some of the packages from my arms. "Don't peek," I said. He grinned and said he wouldn't. I saw him eyeing the large bag holding his jacket. He asked what it was. "I'm not telling," I said playfully. The bag had the name of the man's clothing store written on it.

"I know a guy who works there," he said frowning. "He's a womanizer." What did the guy look like who helped you?" He was studying my face as if looking for a sign of guilt. I thought fast and foolishly told him a woman had helped me. He looked only slightly relieved.

Once I had put the packages away, I went into my office to check my phone messages. I returned a few of the calls then shut it down for the day. I was tired from the hours of shopping yet energized by the time I had with Myla. We had fun; shopping, talking, laughing. Myla was beautiful in every way; full of grace. I knew I would do whatever I could to keep her safe. I asked God repeatedly to protect my children.

It was a Friday, which meant I would be cooped up with him for the next two days. I missed the pre-Joe days when I looked forward to the weekends. I felt gloomy as I walked down the hall and into the living room. I stopped in my tracks when I saw Joe standing in the living room wearing the new jacket. He was looking at himself in the mirror. "Joe!" I shouted. "What are you doing?"

With a startled look, he spluttered, "I knew you bought me a jacket, I could tell by the box. I just wanted to make sure it fit so you wouldn't feel bad if it didn't. It's too big." His words tumbled out so quickly I could hardly understand him.

I looked at the jacket carefully. It fit perfectly, and I told him so. "I wanted it to be a surprise," I said in a tone that I hoped conveyed sad disappointment, but not anger.

"I don't actually like surprises," he snapped. He took the jacket off and stuffed it back into the bag. "It's a nice jacket but I don't like the way it fits. Do you have the receipt?" He looked at me with what I had come to recognize as dangerous eyes.

"Yeah, of course I have the receipt."

"Let's go back to the store. I'm sure the woman who helped you will still be there," he said with a sinister tone.

"Sure," I said without hesitation. I had to give a flawless performance at that point. I didn't want him to know I had lied about a woman helping me. I had to try and stay a step ahead of him.

He looked surprised, even a little disappointed, at my response.

"We'll go after supper. Let's order Chinese food," he suggested. *Thank you God, thank you, thank you, thank you, I love you.* I went into the kitchen, phoned in our order then poured myself a glass of wine. My hands were shaking as I poured. I leaned against the counter, swallowed two big gulps and took a long, deep breath. I couldn't let him see I was nervous or he would conduct a long interrogation.

After a few moments to myself, I joined him in the living room. His eyes were glued to the television. I felt a little calmer. I told myself if he still wanted to go to the store after dinner, the handsome young guy who sold me the jacket would probably be gone. At least I hoped so. I hoped Joe would drop the whole thing. The jacket fit him. It looked nice on him. He knew it.

He was testing me to see how I'd respond to returning it.

I'm not sure if it was stress or the food, but I started feeling sick shortly after eating. I spent most of the evening in the bathroom. I felt horrible. Joe was actually quite compassionate. He went to the store and bought me ginger ale, which I couldn't keep down. He helped me get into bed, put extra blankets over me and even placed a bucket by the bed. He slept on the couch that night claiming he had a weak stomach. I was too sick to enjoy his absence.

The next day I felt only slightly better. I was in bed almost asleep when he came in and told me he was going out to get a few things. He said he'd buy some chicken noodle soup for me.

As soon as I heard him leave I got up and peeked out the window. I saw him in the parking lot walking towards his car. He was holding the bag the leather jacket was in. *He's the sick one.* I stumbled back into bed and cried myself to sleep. I hadn't been sleeping long when the phone woke me up. I didn't answer it. A few minutes later it rang again. I knew it was him. I answered.

"Hello," I said weakly.

"I'm at the mall. I took the jacket back," he said sharply.

"Did you?"

"Yeah, I did, and I talked to a guy working there. He said he remembers you because you were overly friendly. What the hell's going on?"

"Nothing is going on. I have no idea what you're talking about. I didn't talk to any guy there." I sighed. I felt dizzy and rested my head in my hand.

"I'm going to get to the bottom of this," he declared.

"The bottom of what?" I asked innocently.

"Why he'd tell me that?"

"I don't know; maybe he's confused." *Why are you so fucking crazy?* "Joe, I'm sick as a dog. I have to lie down."

"I'll be home soon," he said, sounding deflated.

I went into the kitchen, poured myself a glass of ginger ale then lay down on the couch. The beautiful afghan my mom had made for me was hanging over the back of the couch. I grabbed on to it and pulled it to my face. I inhaled deeply in search of her scent. I longed to go back in time and be with her. I didn't have the strength to worry about what was going to happen when he got home. I predicted he would keep his distance since he was so paranoid about catching what I had. I told myself I should puke on him. The thought made me smile.

I was watching a rerun of *Cheers* when he got home. He asked me why I wasn't in bed. I told him I needed to stay awake or I'd be up all night. He came over and put his hand on my forehead. "You're a little hot," he determined. "You don't look good, you're really pale. You should probably be in bed."

I got up slowly and went back to bed. I liked the idea of being somewhere he wasn't. A few minutes later he brought the afghan in and tossed over me.

"Tomorrow I'll wash all the bedding," he stated. I was slightly amused because I figured it was killing him not to be interrogating me about the salesman from the store. I was also relieved. Thank you stomach flu! I snuggled into the blankets and relaxed. My stomach felt better, but I definitely wasn't going to admit that.

I spent the rest of the weekend in bed. He kept his distance. Monday morning he rushed out to work. As soon as he left I went to the kitchen and made myself scrambled eggs and toast. I was starving. I milked my flu symptoms for a few more days. It felt like a vacation, but like all vacations, it had to come to an end. Christmas was creeping up and I had many contracts to get done for New Year's Eve bookings. I was happy to keep busy.

Joe had decided he would look for a leather jacket after Christmas when they were on sale. I bought him a shirt and a couple pair of socks just so he would have something from me to open Christmas morning.

We were invited to spend Christmas Eve at his parent's house. We were also invited to a New Year's party at Carrie and Ken's. Joe didn't want to go to Carrie and Ken's, which was for the best. I could well imagine how things would go when a crowd of people began exchanging hugs and kisses. For me, it would be a disaster. I tried not to dwell on all the things I was missing out on; I had to focus on being safe.

Late one afternoon a few days before Christmas, my friends Diane and Faye dropped in. Joe was at work. I hadn't seen them since I'd started working from home, and I was pleased they'd taken the time to pay me a surprise visit. But I was also nervous that Joe would come home. He would find some preposterous excuse to be upset because I had company. I made us each a rum and eggnog and tried to appear as though I was enjoying the visit. My stomach was in knots. When I heard a car door shut, I jumped up and looked out the window. It wasn't him. Diane asked me if everything was okay. I had to come up with something; I was so worried he would walk in. I could picture him calling me into the other room and ordering me to get rid of them so we could talk. I could picture the interrogation, the lecture, the beating. I could feel it. I told them Joe was picking me up shortly to go Christmas shopping. "He's leaving work early so I probably should start getting ready," I said, avoiding their eyes. "I'm so sorry to cut our visit short."

They understood. We hugged and wished each other a happy Christmas. As soon as they left I tidied up, brushed my teeth and went back to typing contracts. I felt a dark sense of loneliness wash over me. Joe had called me earlier to say he was bringing fish and chips home for supper. I was glad I didn't have to cook. Lately, he criticized everything I made. It was one more opportunity for him to make me feel inadequate. I had a hard time concentrating on my work. I couldn't stop wishing I was out with my friends, having a few drinks and lots of laughs, wishing I could do whatever I wanted, whenever I wanted. I was imprisoned by fear; he didn't even have to be physically present to guard me.

We had dinner at his parent's place on Christmas Eve. Both of his brothers were there with their wives and kids. They were nice people. It was obvious to me the wives weren't afraid of their husbands. I wondered if they could tell I was afraid of Joe. I felt extremely uncomfortable. I was glad when Joe wanted to leave right after dinner.

As soon as we got home, he insisted I open my presents. He handed them to me one at a time. The first gift I opened was a pair of black patent shoes. The next was a pretty knitted dress. I really liked the colour of it; a silvery-grey. He also gave me a pair of sparkling silver earrings, perfume, bath oils, lotions and a black silk nightgown. The last gift he handed was tiny — the size of a ring box. That's exactly what it was; exactly what I was afraid of. Inside was a beautiful diamond ring. I acted surprised to hide my alarm. He got down on one knee and proposed. He had tears in his eyes; so did I when I said yes. *How dare he do this to me? He knows I'm too fucking scared to say no.* He threw his arms around me, "You've made me the happiest man in the world," he gushed. I felt like the saddest woman in the world faking happiness so she wouldn't get the crap beaten out of her. That's what I felt like.

Christmas day was a blur. Joe intentionally delayed us; he took an extra long shower, pretended he couldn't find his car keys, phoned his parents and chatted. We arrived embarrassingly late. Everyone had opened their gifts. As soon as we finished handing out our gifts, Joe stood up and announced our engagement. I showed everyone my ring. "It's beautiful, congratulations," I heard over and over again.

Joe was on his best behaviour and was really sociable until someone suggested we should pick teams and have a dart tournament. Then he became clingy. Each of us drew a piece of paper with a number written on it. The even numbers were on one team and odd numbers on the other. I picked an even number and Joe picked an odd number. Brad, Myla's boyfriend, had also picked an even number. Joe persuaded him to trade. I could tell Brad didn't care which team he played on, no one did except Joe. I saw Chad look at Myla and roll his eyes. I imagined everyone was thinking the same thing. I laughed in the hopes of making it seem more amusing than anything else. Before long everyone was having a good time playing darts in a friendly competition. The odd number team won. I was happy because it was the team Chad and Myla were on.

Everyone pitched in to prepare dinner. It was a delicious feast. Surrounded by my family, I felt more relaxed than I had been for a long time. Not long after we finished dinner Joe wanted to go to bed. I was in the middle of a conversation with Chad and my brother when he interrupted me to request we go to our room. He claimed he didn't feel well.

"You don't have to go with him, Mom, you should stay. You've haven't had much time with Grandma," Chad said a little impatiently. "Joe can go to the room by himself. He's a big boy."

I felt Joe's tension, but it wasn't as powerful as usual. I invited Joe to stay up a little longer because I knew he wouldn't leave me alone with my family. He pretended he had changed his mind and joined me at the table my mom and sister-in-law were sitting at. Joe was charming as could be, which I was thankful for. The last thing I wanted was for Mom to be concerned about me.

Later, while I was in the washroom, my sister-in-law came in. She asked me if I was happy.

I told her I was. "He seems pretty controlling, Leah," she said boldly. "Yeah, he is kind of controlling, but he's working on it," I said as convincingly as I could.

We were the first to go bed that evening and the first to leave the next day. I got tears in my eyes when I said goodbye to my mom. I couldn't stop wondering if I would ever see her again, not because I feared something might happen to her, but because I was afraid something might happen to me.

We spent the next day watching movies. It was a peaceful way to pass the time. The day after that, Joe returned to work. I didn't have much work to do because my buyers weren't interested in booking anything until after New Year's Eve. I was tidying up my office when the phone rang. It was Myla. She and Chad wanted me to meet them for lunch. I talked them into coming over.

"I have left-over lasagne and garlic bread," I offered.

"Is Joe at work?" Myla asked. I told her he was and she said they would be right over.

We ate lunch and visited. Myla and her friend Nicole had a trip to Jamaica planned. She brought her itinerary along and we spent most of the time looking through it. It was fun to share in her excitement. The subject of my so-called engagement didn't come up. Just before they left, Chad looked at me seriously and said, "Mom you sure were quiet at Christmas. Usually you're the life of the party." Both kids looked at me as though they were searching my face for an explanation. *Please God, don't let them see my guilt and shame.*

"Sorry about that. I was so bloody tired. We were up until about three in the morning on Christmas Eve," I calmly explained. It was the truth; we were up late because he needed to talk about our engagement and how much it meant to him. It had been a strain convincing him it meant just as much to me.

"Why were you up so late?" Myla asked.

"We got home from Joe's parents and decided to open presents, next thing we knew it was three in the morning," I said without making eye contact.

I was too angry to cry after they left. I was constantly covering up for him; for him and me, actually. I was telling lies and that made me a liar. I felt corrupt. I felt worthless. I felt hopeless. I couldn't get Chad and Myla's faces out of my head. *They deserve so much better than me for a mother.* My heart ached; I was in excruciating emotional pain.

All my regrets ganged up and tackled me. I went into my bedroom and lay down. I reminded myself of the times, early in the relationship, when I should have ended it. I reminded myself I was doing nothing to get away from him. I had chickened out of opening my own bank account because I couldn't bring myself to ask Myla if I could use her address. I had no right to involve her in any of this. I wished Joe would die. It was something I'd been wishing almost constantly, and it scared me to have such thoughts. *Was I just as bad as he was?*

Joe made dinner reservations for New Year's Eve. I felt surprisingly relaxed getting ready that evening. It was New Year's Eve after all. The end of a year I couldn't wait to say goodbye to, and the beginning of a year I wanted to greet with hope. I spent a lot of time getting ready. Once I had my hair done and makeup applied, I put on the dress he had bought me for Christmas. I studied my reflection. I hadn't noticed how nicely it fit when I tried it on Christmas Eve. It looked so plain and proper on the hanger which, I figured, was why he chose it for me. I smiled to myself. He was ready and waiting in the living room. I strolled into the room expecting him to suggest I wear something else, but he didn't. He told me I looked sexy and beautiful. He said he was the luckiest man in the world. I smiled and thanked him. "You only have eyes for me, right baby?" he asked anxiously.

Sometimes I felt sorry for him. It was one of those times, and I was surprised at how deeply I felt his pain. "Right baby," I said softly. His face lit up. He walked over to me, lifted my hand and kissed it gently. Those times were extremely confusing for me. I didn't understand how or why I could feel compassion and possibly even love for him.

He was a great companion that evening. It reminded me of our early dates and why I had fallen head over heels for him. We left the restaurant hand in hand. As soon as we got home he poured us each a glass of champagne. He toasted me as his future wife. I smiled and secretly made a wish that he was my future ex-boyfriend. *Unless he stays the way he is right now.* By midnight we were both giddy from the champagne. We toasted 1995.

"Nineteen ninety four was the best year of my life because it's the year I met you," he said passionately. I knew he expected me to say it was my best year too. The thought was so absurd I started to giggle. "What are you laughing at?"

"I'm sorry. I'm tipsy and you look so cute," I said, thinking as fast as I could. He relaxed, put his arm around me and kissed my cheek. I gave my fear and struggle for dignity some time off as he continued kissing me; my face, my lips, my neck. His hands wandered over my body and under my dress. Not even my mind resisted. "I love you," I whispered. *Just for this moment.*

"I love you too, sweet pea. I love you more than my first breath. Let's go to bed." I followed him to the bedroom. My body craved fulfillment. I didn't judge myself or him that night. It felt so normal to be a couple making love.

Chapter 17

NEW YEAR'S DAY, he got up early and made pancakes and bacon. I just wanted to sleep but I dragged myself to the table and forced down one pancake and a piece of bacon. He looked offended when I refused to have more. I explained I was suffering from too much champagne.

"It wasn't cheap champagne," he said defensively.

"I know it wasn't. I'm just not used to champagne; I think I've only had it a couple times in my life," I said.

"It's early, go back to bed for awhile."

I took a couple aspirin and retreated back to bed. I went right to sleep and slept for nearly two hours. He woke me up with gentle kisses on my forehead.

"Wake up sleeping beauty," he hummed. "I have a surprise for you."

"What time is it?" I asked rubbing my eyes.

"It's almost eleven. Do you want to see what the surprise is?" He had a childish expression on his face.

I sat up straight and instructed myself to act thrilled with his surprise. He escorted me out of bed and led me into my office. He had completely rearranged the room. Basically everything that had been against the north wall was now against the south wall and vice versa. My desk was still in the same place but the top of it was cleared of everything except the phone. "Come here," he said motioning me over to the desk. He opened a drawer to show me where he had stored my stapler, pens, paper clips and notepads.

"What do you think?" he asked, looking very proud of himself.

"I like it. Thank you Joe." *I hate it. Leave my stuff alone!* I gave him a hug and told myself it could be worse. *At least he's in a good mood.*

When he finally stopped admiring his redecorating I went and had a shower. When I got out he suggested we invite Myla and Chad over for dinner. He said he'd make roast chicken. I liked the idea, especially since he was in such good spirits. I would have invited them ahead of time but I was so unsure of what each day might bring. I had learned not to plan ahead. Everything in my life depended on him; his mood. I called them right away. They both declined for the same reason; they had partied too much the night before. I was disappointed but I understood, and in a way I was relieved that I didn't have to worry all day about how Joe might act. I wished them each a happy new year and advised them to drink lots of water and get plenty of rest.

"Thanks, Dr. Mom," Myla said. I chuckled even though I could feel tears welling in my eyes. I hung up and went into the bathroom for some privacy. I sat down and tried to stop myself from crying. I was terrified I was going to lose my kids. They were going to see through my facade of a life. I knew after Christmas they didn't feel the same way about Joe. I wondered how they felt about me. Disappointed, I suspected. *I'll find a way out and I'll never tell anyone what happened.* I jumped when he knocked on the door.

"Are you okay?"

"I'm fine; I'll be out in a minute." I flushed the toilet for effect then washed my hands. When I opened the door he was standing there. "Oh wow, a line up," I joked to conceal my annoyance.

"I have to go," he stated as he rushed past me. I wondered how long he'd been standing outside the door. I could picture him with his ear pressed against the door, listening for God knows what.

I heard him running the shower as I made myself a piece of toast. I was glad to have him out of my hair. I poured a cup of coffee and sat down at the table. I dreaded the day ahead and I resented the pleasure I felt the night before. *How could I have wanted to make love with a man who beats me? What was wrong with me?* My life was so sick and twisted;

I could barely stand living it. I managed to take a couple bites of the toast then threw the rest in the garbage.

I got through the day by staying busy. I indulged in a long bath, did some laundry, and re-read a magazine article. Then I watched Joe's favourite Colonel Custer movie with him. It was about the fifth time I had seen it, so my mind wandered. I wondered what exactly it was about this movie that intrigued Joe so much. I understood his interest in mafia movies since he imagined he was a member, but I couldn't put my finger on what grabbed him in this movie. Was it the unconditional love he perceived Custer's wife had for him, or was it something about the Colonel himself, perhaps his position of power? I told myself it would take a team of psychiatrists to understand what Joe thought about anything or everything.

After the movie, we made dinner. At first Joe objected to my helping. He said I should relax and let him cook for his Princess Leah. "The princess is bored," I said. "I'll make the potatoes and salad; you do the rest, how's that?" He agreed.

We were working side by side in the kitchen listening to music when he said he had something to talk to me about after dinner. I hated hearing those words from him; they always lead to other words I didn't want to hear.

My mom phoned to wish us a happy new year and so did my brother. My brother, with his gift of the gab, kept me on the phone for ages. Every time I laughed at something he said, Joe gave me a dirty look. Worried my laughter would provoke something, I told my brother I had to run. Finally we sat down to eat. It was a nice meal, one that should have been enjoyed, but I had a difficult time eating. Joe had been quiet since I talked to my brother, and I could only imagine the sick thoughts going through his sick head.

"What were you guys laughing about on the phone?"

"He was telling me about their new year's party. One of their neighbours got pretty loaded and said he was going home. Everyone was downstairs in the family room. They saw him climb the stairs and didn't think anymore about him. When my brother and Deanna went to get ready for bed they found him in their bed, sound asleep." I chuckled as I told him the story. He didn't look amused.

"Are you sure you weren't laughing about me," he inquired with a suspicious glare.

"We weren't laughing about you. Why would you think that?"

"I heard my name."

"He asked me what we did last night and I told him you and I went out for dinner." I explained, hating the uneasiness I felt. My hands started trembling. I put them in my lap so he couldn't see them. Trembling hands, in his opinion, would be proof I was lying. "The chicken is delicious," I said.

"Thanks," he replied in a softer tone. He took a mouthful, chewed it slowly then said, "I have to admit, it is good."

I calmed myself down enough to continue eating. I ate, tiny bites, wishing it was later than six-thirty. I wished it was late at night and he was sleeping. I wished I could fall asleep and wake up in a new life. As soon as we finished dinner he went into the living room for a cigarette. I cleared the table, loaded the dishwasher, wiped the counters, washed pots and pans and put away the leftovers. I couldn't quite shake my uneasiness. I took a few deep breaths as I wiped the counter for the second time.

The phone rang. I heard him rushing to answer it. I heard him curtly tell the caller I was having a bath. I turned the dishwasher on, went into the living room and asked him who had called. He said it was Carrie.

"Why did you tell her I was having a bath?" I asked trying my best to hide my anger. I was concerned with the way he talked to Carrie. I knew she would have wished him a happy new year and I knew he didn't acknowledge it. He was rude to her. *Poor Carrie.*

"You've been on the phone almost all day and I'm tired of it. This is our time. I told you I wanted to talk to you about something. Unless you think talking to Carrie is more important than talking to me." He was on the verge of exploding.

"Talking to you is more important than talking to anyone else," I said, fully aware I was patronizing him. *I hope he chokes on his words.* I saw his face relax a little. He sat down in his favourite chair. As soon as I sat down on the couch he started. "Leah, I'm making a rule that your kids and friends can call you when I'm at work, but when I'm home it's our time. Do you understand?"

"I understand." *I understand you're one sick son of a bitch.* "My mom, my brother and Carrie called to wish us a happy new year that's all. I called my kids; remember, to invite them for dinner." I spoke kindly even though I felt like a complete fool for participating in such an outrageous conversation. I wanted to protest, loudly and strongly. But I knew if I resisted at all, he would retaliate and get his own way. I told myself I'd deal with it later, but for now I should just do what I needed to avoid a night of horror.

"I have lots of friends, Leah, they don't call here. They know this is our time; that's respect.

My brothers know I don't like to be bothered when I'm with you; that's respect. My parents only phone to invite us over, not to interrupt our private time; that's respect." He put on an Italian accent when he said, that's respect.

I nodded meekly. I couldn't help wondering if he actually thought I believed he had lots of friends or that the only reason his brothers never phoned him was out of respect. As far as his parents went, they rarely called him and he rarely called them. I didn't blame them. I didn't blame them for anything; it was impossible to have a normal relationship with him. I figured they had probably tried.

"You better put an end to all these phone calls, Leah. I mean it; I'm putting my foot down." I knew he was looking for an excuse to start something with me. I could see it in his dilated eyes; a craving for his power fix. My mind searched desperately for the right words to diffuse the situation. I wanted to tell him he had no friends because he was an asshole. I wanted to tell him I hated him and I wanted him out of my life. *Just think it; don't say it. Agree with him. It's the only way to protect yourself.* "I will, Joe. Don't worry about it. If anyone else calls we'll let the machine get it," I said in the most convincing voice I could summon.

He sat silently with a blank look on his face. I began wishing with every ounce of my being that his parents would phone. Like magic, the phone rang. I froze. He jumped up quickly and answered it gruffly. I watched him as the expression on his face changed from self-serving agitation to humiliation. I knew instantly it was his mom or dad. He mumbled a new year's greeting then cruelly said we were busy and hung up. "My parents are fucking idiots," he announced as he stomped away from the phone. *You're the fucking idiot!*

"It's nice they were thinking about you," I said holding my satisfaction inside. He didn't respond. A few minutes later he marched into the kitchen and made himself a rum and coke. He asked me if I wanted a glass of wine. I definitely did. When he returned with the drinks I thanked him. He didn't answer. He was pouting. He turned the television on, checked a few channels, sighed with disappointment then turned it off. I could feel the wheels turning in his menacing mind. I got up and turned the radio on. I needed sound. I needed harmony. "That's too loud," he complained. I lowered the volume. "Leah, I want to set a date for our wedding. I want to get married on Valentine's Day," he said searching my face for clues of rejection. My legs felt weak. I didn't know what to say. "What's wrong?" he asked loudly.

"Nothing, you caught me off guard that's all." I could feel my heart racing and my body heating up.

"We'll get married on Valentine's Day." It quickly occurred to me that he had told me he and Julia were married on Valentine's Day. *What an arrogant bastard.*

"That's the day you married Julia. I don't want get married on your anniversary," I said, grateful to have a way out. I was terrified if I set a date to marry him he would make sure it happened. The thought of marrying him was too much. I couldn't stand it. He looked surprised; perhaps he had forgotten about marrying Julia on Valentine's Day.

"That was a mistake, it doesn't count," he stuttered. "She conned me into marrying her, I didn't love her. The fucking bitch ruined Valentine's Day for us."

I wondered what he had done to Julia. I wondered where she was and if she was okay. He was staring at me. *I'd better say the right thing.* "I'd rather have a summer wedding," I said looking directly into his harsh eyes, the way he had taught me to do. "We could have an outdoor wedding. It would be easier for my mom to travel in the summer." I knew I was rambling. "There's no rush, Joe, it's not like I'm pregnant," I said, hoping a little humour would lighten him up. He wasn't amused.

"I don't want to wait, and we don't need a big wedding. It's not like it's your first one for Christ sakes. We'll go to the justice of the peace next week and get married." He was waving his hands in the air and talking rapidly. "You better not be giving me the run around."

I didn't know what to say. Part of me thought I should let it go and think up an excuse tomorrow, but another part of me was terrified to agree to it, even for a few hours.

"I don't want to get married right now, Joe," I said firmly.

"Why?"

I took a deep breath. "I'm scared," I admitted. I felt my eyes fill with tears. "I want to wait."

"Why don't you want to marry me, Leah?" he yelled. I looked at him glaring at me and I couldn't stand it. I couldn't do it anymore. He was destroying me and I wasn't doing anything to stop it. I had to try. I couldn't hold the hurt and fear inside me any longer.

"I don't want to marry you because you abuse me." The words poured out of me with painful determination to salvage my shattered spirit. He looked at me with a stunned expression. I felt a glimmer of victory and an infusion of self-respect, but only briefly. He sprung off the chair and flew across the room like a predator going for the kill. He jumped on me, shoved me over and pounded my face with his open hand. I tried to push him off. It was useless. I was helpless. I started to howl and beg him to get off me. "Please Joe. Let's talk, please."

He started yelling and calling me the usual insulting names. At one point he shook me so hard I was afraid my neck was going to snap. He finally released me then ordered me to get off his furniture. I took my position on the floor. I sat there silently scolding myself for opening my big mouth. He was roaring at the top of his lungs. *Somebody please hear this and call the police, please, somebody*. I had wondered many times if my neighbours could hear him. It was a quiet building; loud noise wasn't common. The people who lived next were an older couple, I assumed they didn't hear or didn't want to get involved. I wanted to get to know them but I was too ashamed to make the effort. I figured they didn't realize I needed help; that they could save me just by phoning the police. They probably thought I was a fool who lived with a lunatic.

"You thought you looked so fucking great last night in the dress I bought you. You didn't look good at all, you stupid, ugly slut. You're an ungrateful bitch!" His face was full of hatred. "I shopped for days to find you the perfect gifts for Christmas and you . . . you buy me a cheap fucking shirt. I hate your fucking guts. You women are all the same, you, Lisa and Julie." He pointed his finger at me. "You're the worst of all."

I sat there trying to block his bellowing words from entering my heart. I reminded myself over and over again he was the crazy one. I pictured how he'd be behaving the next day; crying and begging for forgiveness. *Just hate him.*

He stood up and stomped over to the fireplace. I watched him build a fire. I wondered if he wanted a distraction to calm himself down. I hoped with all my might that's what he was doing. Once the fire was going he sat down and watched it for a few minutes. Then he turned to me. "I'm going to teach you lesson," he said with an evil smirk. He stood up then ordered me to do the same. My heart was pounding frantically. "Come with me," he said. He went to the bedroom and opened the closet door. I was behind him, baffled and scared out of my mind. He started pulling my clothes off the hangers and throwing them at me. He ordered me to pick them up. I thought this was an elaborate scheme to make me think he was kicking me out. This went on until I couldn't hold any more. He shoved me back out to the living room and told me to drop everything on the floor. Then he took me back to the closet and piled the rest of my clothes into my arms. I felt torturous humiliation and self-loathing standing there so obediently.

"What are you doing, Joe?" I asked timidly.

"You'll see," he growled.

After dumping the second armful of clothes on the living room floor, he told me to make him a drink. "You better make yourself one too; you're going to need it." He laughed uproariously. I returned to the living room with the drinks. He was standing in front of the fireplace holding the dress he had bought me. I gasped in disbelief as he threw it into the fire. He picked up another item, my favourite black dress, and threw that in too.

"You care more about your fucking clothes than you care about me. You don't deserve to have anything nice. You're an ingrate, Leah, a fucking, lying ingrate. I'm sick of your games." He continued ranting and raving his insults at me while tossing blouses, skirts and pants into the flames. It smelled horrible. The more items he threw into the fire the bigger the flame got, and that seemed to intrigue him. "This works better than wood," he laughed. I couldn't believe what I was seeing. I was petrified he was going to shove me into the fire too. I tried to block out the thought. I knew if I tried to escape he would catch me. Then things would be worse than they already were. *He'll shove me in the fire. He'd love to disfigure me. Maybe he's going shove my face into the flames. I turned to God; Dear God, please, please help me.*

At one point he noticed that the leather chair by the fireplace felt hot. He ordered me to get a spray bottle, fill it with cold water and mist the chair as he continued his burning spree. I was saving his chair while he was destroying my belongings, and there was nothing I could do about it. My spirit was in agony. I looked at the shrinking pile of clothes on the floor and saw the beautiful outfit Myla had bought me. I whimpered. I wanted to save it. He picked it up. "Myla gave me that," I said imploringly.

"You fucking bitch. You didn't say a word when I burned the clothes I bought you. They mean nothing to you." I could tell he took extra pleasure in destroying Myla's gift. I wished I hadn't said anything. I could feel my skin crawling. I didn't know how much more I could take. I felt I was going to shatter into a million pieces.

It took close to two hours to destroy my clothes. My legs were barely holding me up and my head was throbbing. I felt I might pass out from the stench and the heat. He went back into the bedroom and came out holding the photo of my dad I had on my dresser. He'd taken it out of the frame. He held it out to me. I took it. *I love you, Daddy, oh Daddy.* Suddenly his fingers were gripping my wrist; he yanked me over to the fire and held my hand over the hot flame. "Drop it," he yelled, tightening his grip.

I dropped it and watched the fire devour it. *Dear God please protect me, don't let him burn me."*

"You burned your dad's picture. He wouldn't be very proud of you right now, would he?" he taunted. I couldn't stop myself; I cried out a protest. Tears poured down my face. He grabbed me and pushed me around the room until I lost my balance and landed on the floor. He pounced on top of me and started choking me until I almost passed out. Then he hit me over and over again across my head, my ears and my face. I could taste blood. Before he climbed off he added what had become his ultimate act of insult — spitting in my face. I struggled up from the floor. I was dizzy. I was so frightened I thought I'd go out of my mind. He told me to get my coat on and get the hell out. I stood frozen. He brought me my coat. "Put it on or I'll fucking kill you," he said.

Trembling, I put it on. He pointed to the door and told me to go. I wished for nothing more than to walk out, but I'd been through this sick game of his too many times. I told him I didn't want to go. "Get out!" he roared. He grabbed the sleeve of my jacket and yanked me over to the door. "Go!" he ordered. I stood in front of the door. I knew he wasn't going to let me leave, but I thought if I could get the door open maybe someone would be out there, walking down the hallway. Maybe they would help me; rescue me. I grabbed the door handle and turned it frantically. I felt his hand grab the back of my jacket. He yanked me back, shoved me against the wall then ploughed his knee into my stomach. I slide to the floor. He stood over me and walloped me in the face so hard I thought he had broken my nose. I could feel and smell the blood gushing from it. He ordered me to get into the bathroom and clean up.

I staggered into the bathroom. I took my blood-splattered jacket off, grabbed a cold cloth and sat on the seat of the toilet. Mournful sobs racked my body. Silently I begged God to make him stop. I stayed in the bathroom until I stopped the bleeding. I was beaten up and beaten down. I could barely move. I came out of the bathroom and went into my bedroom. I plopped down, face first on the bed. I was sobbing hysterically by then and didn't hear him come into the room. Before I knew it, he was sitting astride my back. He pressed my head into the pillow so I couldn't move it. I thought he was going to suffocate me. Panicking, I began squirming and kicking. I felt something on the back of my hair. He jumped off me and triumphantly said, "See how sexy you are now with no decent clothes and no long hair." I lifted my head up and looked around at him. In one hand, I saw a pair of scissors. In the other, long strands of hair. I touched the back of my head and felt the large gap where he'd cut a chunk of my hair off. I felt totally defeated.

Chapter 18

THE NEXT FEW days were hazy. I functioned like a robot whose battery was running out. This time he wasn't remorseful; he simply said he had drunk too much and things got out of hand. He promised to buy me new clothes and hair extensions. I fretted over what I'd tell Myla when she asked why I never wore the jacket and pants she bought me. I stewed over how I'd explain my hair. I tried to hide the bald area by pulling the sides of my hair to the back and fastening it with a beret. It looked normal from the front but was a mess at the back. He'd cut it so close to the scalp I figured I'd have to get my head shaved to even out the lengths. I decided to let it grow a few inches before getting it cut. I was overwhelmed. I didn't know what to do.

My body and mind were shrouded with shame. I became obsessed with finding ways to hide the truth from the people I loved. I phoned Carrie and told her that when I was blow-drying my hair, some of it got caught in the dryer and I had to cut it out. I told my daughter the same story. The idea came to me because I knew someone it had happened to. "Joe wants to buy me hair extensions," I shamefully boasted

Joe stayed home from work for two days following the ordeal. He said he didn't feel well. I knew he was staying home to keep a close eye on me. It was torture being around him. The only thing I was thankful for was that he didn't bring up marriage. I swore to myself I was not going to marry him.

He went to work on the third day. I sat in the living room after he left and stared at the door, trying to visualize myself walking out of it. I was positive he would kill me if I didn't get out soon. I was petrified. I sat there all morning in a state of utter despair.

Late that afternoon, Myla phoned. I could barely hold back my tears when I heard her voice. She reminded me she and Nicole were leaving for their Jamaican vacation in two days. She wanted to get together before she left. I felt terrible because I thought they weren't leaving for another week. I told her I had lost track of time; she just laughed. She said Chad was working evenings so they were meeting for lunch the next day. I suggested they come to my place, but she said they really wanted to go out. I told her I'd call her in the morning to set things up. I told her I loved her and couldn't wait to see her and Chad.

I promised myself I was going; I felt a tinge of strength just thinking it. I wondered what I was going to wear. The only clothes I had left were the few things in my dresser drawer and the T-shirt and jeans I was wearing the night he burned my belongings. I looked through my drawers. I had socks, underwear, a sweat shirt and two winter sweaters. The sweaters were old but in good shape. I decided I would wear the dark-blue sweater. The sleeves were extra long and would cover the bruises on my arms and hands.

Joe came home shortly after my conversation with Myla. He said he was tired then went into the bedroom to nap. I was in my office trying to focus on the task of filing contracts. I imagined him straining his ears to hear every move I made. I tried not to make a sound he would recognize. He was back in my office within twenty minutes, telling me he was going to order a pizza. I hadn't eaten all day. I had no appetite; the only thing I hungered for was my freedom. When the pizza delivery guy arrived I was in the kitchen. I went to answer the door, but before I could get to the buzzer Joe shot in front of me and answered it. He told me to go into the other room and stay there until the guy left. "I'm not taking any chances of you flirting with him like last time. I want a peaceful night." I had no idea what he was talking about but it didn't matter. It was a long and dreary evening. He watched television. I pretended to watch, but my mind was trying to scheme an escape.

The next morning he got up and showered, as usual, and I made coffee, as usual. After our ritual of my offering and his refusing breakfast, I drank several cups of coffee. I had barely slept the last few nights, so I was relying on caffeine to snap my brain awake. Once the caffeine kicked in, my brain told me to panic. Instead of rushing around, he strolled into the kitchen wearing his robe. I hid my anxiety well when he said he wasn't going into work until later, but when he announced his boss had told him to take the day off, I thought I was going to faint.

I was devastated. I wondered if I should just tell him I was meeting my kids for lunch; a little bon voyage party for Myla. A scenario played through my head; me telling him I was going out to meet them; him, in various ways, making it impossible. I couldn't stop imagining what he might do to me. I didn't put anything past him. He had threatened to kill me so many times: "I'm ready to slit your fucking throat," was one of the threats he particularly relished. I didn't want to die. I had to think of an excuse to get out of meeting my kids. What could I say without hurting their feelings?

I got dressed and went into my office. Joe came in and suggested we go shopping to buy me some new clothes. I didn't want him to buy me anything. Nothing was mine anyway.

"I don't really feel up to going shopping. My back is killing me," I said grimacing. It did not seem to occur to him that I was hurting all over from his brutal beating. A haunting image of my body huddled on the floor while he hit, punched, kicked and choked me into submission flashed through my mind.

"Take some aspirin," he snapped.

"I did all ready," I said. *Drop dead you fucking asshole.*

"I know what I did the other night was wrong, but at least I didn't break anything," he had the nerve to say.

"You could have," I blurted out.

"But I didn't and I wouldn't," he bragged. He had said the same thing to me many times. He stood in the doorway looking at me as if he expected applause. His robe was open showing his army-green boxers and the stupid white undershirt. His hair was uncombed and his face unshaven. He looked ugly and mean.

The phone rang and I jumped. I grabbed it quickly. It was Myla. "Hi Mom, how are you?"she asked brightly. My heart began to pound as I told her I was on the other line and would get back to her. It was the first thing that popped into my head.

"Who was that?" Joe demanded.

"It was Myla," I said, then immediately wished I had told him it was someone else.

"Why did you lie to her? Why didn't you just tell her you were talking to me?" His voice and body language were confrontational.

"I don't know. I guess because of what we were talking about. It was stupid, I shouldn't have lied to her, it's not as if she would have asked what we were talking about," I said. "She's not snoopy." *Like you.*

"Call her back. Tell her it's our time together and you'll phone her tomorrow, when I'm at work," he ordered.

"I'll call her later. I think she wants a little mother-daughter talk. She's leaving for Jamaica on Thursday," I said, hoping he would back off. I wasn't going to willingly phone her and pass on his orders.

"You can have your mother-daughter talk tomorrow when I'm not around. I stayed home to spend time with you. We'll invite her over when she gets back. This is our time together, Leah, and your kids better respect that. I told you I'm putting my foot down. Either you phone her or I will."

I didn't want him phoning Myla; that would crush her even more than I was going to. He walked over to the front of my desk and stood there with his hands folded in front of him. "I mean it," he said through gritted teeth.

"I'm not telling her she can't phone here when your home," I boldly told him. He didn't respond. While dialling her number I tried to re-hearse what I would say to her. Nothing made sense. I was coming apart. Her line was busy. *Thank you, God.* I held the phone out so he could hear the busy signal. He grunted and stormed out. I knew he'd be back.

He had barely left the room when the phone rang. It was Myla again. She asked if I was still on the other line. I told her I wasn't and she quickly went on to say Chad would be at her place by noon. She asked me if I'd meet them there. I could feel Joe's evil presence outside the door. *Don't mention lunch. Don't mention lunch.* I promised myself I would make everything up to my children one day.

"Joe took the day off to spend it with me. It was a surprise, so we're going to hang out together today," I said knowing how lame it sounded.

"You're not meeting us for lunch?" she asked, not trying to hide her disappointment and disbelief.

"No, not today but when you get back we'll have you guys over for dinner. You can tell us all about your vacation." I felt like the worst mother in the world.

"Chad is going to be upset, Mom," she said. "Are you sure you want to cancel?"

I felt so left out of their lives. I was left out. Joe was making sure of that. I fought back my tears. "I think I should. I'll call you tomorrow," I said, forcing a cool tone into my voice. I had to get off the phone; he was now in the room glaring at me impatiently. I wanted to scream in agony.

He said he thought I should have explained things more firmly. Apparently he thought I still cared what he thought. I could see right through him; he wanted Chad and Myla out of my life. He wanted me all to himself to abuse without risk of interference. I told myself I could beat him at his sick game, but I wasn't beating him, not yet.

I told him I had to get contracts ready to send by fax." They have to go out today," I said.

It wasn't true but it accomplished getting him out of my office. I couldn't stop thinking about my kids; the hurt and disappointment in Myla's voice. *Things can't go on this way.*

I went to the kitchen for a glass of water. I saw him sitting in the living room watching television. He still wasn't dressed. I considered asking him to go to the store for something so I could phone Myla but then thought he'd probably make me go with him. I hurried back to my office. Every time my phone rang I could feel him more than hear him sneaking down the hallway to listen outside my door. Guy Cool phoned; as usual, he wanted to come by with my commission. I told him I was swamped and he should mail it. I was curt. He sounded let down. Shortly after I talked to Guy, an agent phoned me. He needed a band to go to Vancouver the following week. I called Guy back and asked him if they would be interested in taking the gig. He and his band had planned to take the week off but the offer was too good to pass up. He asked me if he should come over and sign the contract. I told him I had to fax it to the club manager first and probably wouldn't get it back until tomorrow. I could hear my voice quivering as I spoke.

Joe appeared while I was still talking. "You won't get what until tomorrow?" he demanded to know. I looked at him and put my finger up as a signal to wait until I was off the phone. Guy thanked me for the booking. I thanked him for accepting it on his week off.

"I won't get a contract back from Vancouver until tomorrow," I told Joe as I hung up. He had that odd blank look in his eyes I had come to fear.

"What's the contract for?"

It's none of your business you paranoid freak. "I booked a band to play in Vancouver."

"That's good. What band did you book?"

"The Cool Guys," I said, wishing it could have been another band.

"So that's who you were talking to?" he stated like a question. "Guy Cool."

"Yeah," I said feeling my muscles tense. I glanced up at him. He was staring at me fiercely.

"You're too friendly, it's not professional. I knew it. I have to keep my eye on you. I'm quitting my job. I'll work with you. You can teach me how to be an agent and I'll teach you how to behave."

I felt sick with anger. *You're going to teach me how to behave. You, a guy who beats up women is going to teach me how to behave.* I couldn't stand it; I had to say something. "I know how to behave," I said looking into his eyes. I quickly softened my expression as his comment about quitting his job sunk in. The thought of him never leaving my side was too much to deal with. I couldn't chance provoking him. I had to figure out a way to make sure he didn't quit his job. It was the only escape I had from the nightmare.

"I don't think so," he said, then turned and left. I sat there in anguish. I had no idea what to do next. I began praying. *I'm sorry God. I don't know what else to do. I need help. I need help to help myself. Please help me. Please don't let him quit his job.*

A few minutes later there was a knock at the door. I thought it must be someone who lived in the building because I had not heard the buzzer. Joe said something I couldn't make out. Then I heard Chad's voice; he was saying he wanted to talk to me. My mind was in such turmoil, I could hardly believe Chad was here. I sat in stunned silence. The sound of a grunt and someone landing heavily against the wall snapped me out of my inertia. I rushed to the door. I saw Joe pressing his hands against Chad's shoulders trying to keep him from coming in. Chad was push-ing back. Without hesitation I ran back to my office and dialled 911. "I need help right away. My boyfriend is violent. He's trying to hurt my son. He's dangerous, please hurry," I implored. The operator asked me several questions; my name, my address, if there were weapons in the house, how old my son was. She told me to stay on the line. I said I couldn't' and hung up. I had to make sure Chad was okay. I rushed back to the door. Chad was inside and Joe was apologizing to him and making excuses for his behaviour. They had no idea I phoned the police. The phone rang, I answered in the kitchen, it was the 911 operator; she told me to stay on the line. I heard Joe telling Chad he should go. "Please hurry," I begged the 911 operator. She told me to stay on the line. "You don't understand; I have to hang up," I told her again.

I saw the bewildered, angry look on my son's face and I wanted to cry. "Chad, don't go!" I said urgently. "The police are on their way." I took his arm and led him to the couch. I sat right next to him. He put his arm around me protectively and patted my shoulder. He had no idea what he had saved me from.

"I just came over to see you. Myla said you sounded weird on the phone," he said as if he thought he had to explain.

"It's okay, I'm glad you came," I said softly.

"I told Joe I wanted to talk to you for a minute. He said you were busy then tried to shut the door in my face. I wanted to make sure you were okay so I pushed my way in. Why didn't he want me to see you? What's his problem?" He spoke in a hushed tone.

"I don't know what his problem is, Chad." I said in the same hushed tone. Just then Joe came back into the living room. He had changed into a T-shirt and jeans. He sat down on the chair facing us, but I couldn't look at him.

He seemed to think a neighbour had called the police. His belligerence had been replaced by an attempt at reasonableness and contrition He was telling Chad what to say when the police arrived. It was gratifying to see him so nervous.

Two officers arrived within minutes. They talked to Chad and Joe. If Chad had known the truth then, he would have given a different answer to the police when they asked him if he wanted to press charges. I heard Joe telling the officers that Chad was a good kid and it was just a misunderstanding. I looked over at Chad; I could tell he didn't know what to say or do. I knew exactly how he felt. It didn't take long for the police to be satisfied that the situation was diffused. They were about to leave. Once convinced I was okay, Chad was also going to leave. I couldn't bear the thought of him leaving. *What if I never see him again?*

I realized this was the opportunity I had been waiting and praying for, and that I might never get this chance again. *Leave before it's too late.*

"Would you escort me out of here?" I asked the police in desperation.

The officer readily consented and said I should grab a few belongings to take with me. I rushed into my bedroom and grabbed an overnight bag. I emptied my underwear drawer into the bag, grabbed my makeup, a sweat shirt and my address book. Joe tried to follow me down the hall. One of the officers ordered him to sit down. When I got back to the living room, Joe was obediently sitting on a chair. He looked small.

Jumping up, he cried, "Don't do this, Leah. Stay, we'll talk." I ignored him. "Give me back the ring!" he demanded.

"Sit down and shut up!" the officer told Joe firmly. It was an astonishing thing to witness. "How does it feel to be intimidated?" I said to him a little smugly as I watched him sink back down into the chair. He looked away. I took my ring off and tossed it on the table before we walked out.

Part III

Chapter 19

I FELT EXHILARATED WALKING out that day, but the feeling didn't last long. Chad took me to his apartment. He was still seething and asked me repeatedly why I hadn't thrown Joe out ages ago. I phoned Myla and told her to come over right away. It seemed to take forever for her to get there. Hideous things went through my head as I waited — I imagined Joe going to her apartment, attacking her. When she finally arrived, I told her what had happened at my apartment.

"I'm finished with him. Who does he think he is, trying to keep my kids away from me? He's such an idiot; a control freak." I sounded convincingly strong and confident.

"It's your apartment; kick him out," Chad said.

"I will," I said firmly. "But for now, I want to avoid him. I don't want to see him or talk to him. If he calls say you don't know where I am." I had hardly finished my sentence when the phone rang. It was Joe. Chad told him I wasn't there, and when Joe asked him where I was, Chad told him it was none of his business. I shuddered to think how angry he must be. *He's probably planning his revenge against me.*

Since Myla and her roommate were leaving the next day for their vacation, she offered me her apartment. I took her key but I knew I wasn't going there. I had to go somewhere he wouldn't find me. I asked her to stay with me at Chad's that night. She agreed without question. Joe called again. Chad forcefully told him not to call again then slammed the phone down in his ear. I was a nervous wreck by then.

"What's wrong Mom? You're acting like you're terrified. Are you scared of him?" Myla asked anxiously. I pulled myself together; something I had become used to doing.

"I'm not scared of him, but I don't trust him after the way he acted when Chad came over. I was shocked and I didn't know what to do. I can't imagine what made him behave that way, but I'll never go back to him that's for sure." Chad and Myla said "good" at the same time.

It was difficult to keep up the masquerade, but I couldn't tell them about the horrific abuse. I had no idea how to explain the situation. No idea how to explain why I had not left him sooner. I had promised myself many times that I would never tell anyone, especially my kids and my mom, what had happened. They would be heartbroken, disappointed in me, disgusted.

It was a long night. I jumped at every sound. I was constantly looking out the window, even though we were on the fourth floor. Chad ordered a pizza. I was terrified when the delivery guy knocked on the door. *What if Chad opens the door and its Joe standing there?*

I didn't sleep at all that night. Vivid images of Joe's brutality played out like horror movies in my head. By morning, I had decided to ask Aunt Liz if I could stay with her for a few days. Joe had never met her and had no idea where she lived. I called and told her I was having some problems with Joe and just needed to get away for a few days. She assured me I was welcome to stay. As I hung up, I realized I had not spoken to her since the morning after I dreamt about her late husband and my dad. I wished with all my heart I had paid attention to that dream.

Later, Chad and I drove Myla and Nicole to the airport. We had to stop at her place first and pick up her luggage. Then we stopped at my bank. Chad and Myla came in with me. I was nervous withdrawing the balance out of the joint account. It was all my money anyway; he rarely put anything in. I also removed my name from the account, so it took ages. I kept looking over my shoulder expecting to see him barge in and demand I hand over the money. There was a little over nine-hundred dollars in the account. I stuffed it into my purse wondering when I'd be able to get back to my office and take care of my business. I felt sick thinking of him answering my business calls. I could only imagine what he'd be saying to my clients.

After we left the bank we headed straight to the airport. I watched every car we passed or that passed us. I didn't think Joe would even remember it was the day Myla was leaving, but what if he did? What if he was at the airport looking for me? As it turned out I didn't have to go in. We were running late so dropped them off at the door.

On the way to my aunt's, I told Chad that Joe was relentless and would likely call him again and try to win him over with some crazy story. I stressed he should say he didn't know where I was. I ended by apologizing for all the unpleasantness. I hoped I hadn't given away how terrified I was.

"Don't worry, Mom. I haven't liked him for a long time, he's phony. He could never win me over. I'll kick his ass if he comes near me. I'll kick him out of your apartment too," Chad assured me. "If you need my help, just let me know."

"You're helping me right now," I said warmly. After a few moments hesitation, I launched into my official version of why I didn't want to confront Joe. "There's something wrong with him. It took me a long time to see it, but he has a lot of issues. Most people, even if they're upset when a relationship ends, they deal with it. I don't think he can deal with it; it's going to take time. That's why I don't want to see him or talk to him. I need to figure some things out. I'm going to phone all my clients and tell them I'm taking a few days off."

Aunt Liz had her guest room ready for me. I was exhausted. The bed looked so welcoming I couldn't resist it. I slept for an hour. When I got up I made several phone calls to clients. I asked one of my colleagues, another agent in Calgary, if I could use him as a contact for my bands in case they had any problems. He was happy to help and didn't pry. I started to feel less overwhelmed. I had tea with my aunt and explained I had left Joe because of his jealously. She patted my hand and told me I had done the right thing.

"You look drained, just relax. You know you can stay as long as you need to," she said lovingly. I broke down and cried. She reached out and took hold of my hand. I was on the verge of emotional collapse and the only thing holding me together was the warmth of her touch.

Chapter 20

L ATER THAT DAY, I phoned Carrie. As soon as I heard her voice I started to shake. I didn't know what to tell her. I knew Joe would badger her mercilessly, and it was my fault. I brought a psycho into her life. I was fighting back tears while telling her I had left Joe. I told her what happened with Chad.

"Joe's been acting crazy," I said, nervously. "I want to stay away from him right now. Carrie, I'm worried he's going to be phoning you, trying to find out where I am."

"He has, Leah," she said. "I had just hung up when you called. I told him I hadn't heard from you. Why don't you come over later? Ken's working tonight; we can have a good visit."

"I can't. My car is still over at the apartment. I don't want to go and get it in case I run into him. I'll pick it up in a day or two." That was only one of the reasons I didn't want to get my car; I was also afraid he would drive up and down every street in Calgary looking for it.

"I'll pick you up," Carrie offered. "You can stay overnight if you want." My spirits rose at the thought of seeing her. I readily agreed.

Before Carrie picked me up, I phoned my mom and told her my edited version of events. I knew she had her doubts about Joe after his childish behaviour at Christmas, so she was probably relieved I had left him. I knew Joe wouldn't know how to get a hold of her because her number was unlisted. However, I stressed I didn't want him to know where I was.

"He'd pester the hell out of me," I said. I made a couple of jokes about him to minimize her worry then I assured her I was fine and went on to talk about other things.

Carrie's two oldest kids were out for the evening and her two youngest were spending the night at their grandma's. She was excited about our long overdue girl's night. As soon as we got to her place she said she had a little surprise; she went to the fridge and pulled out a bottle of my favourite French wine. "Let's party!" she cheered.

"Alright! I can't remember the last time I had a glass of that wine. I know it was before I met Joe. He always bought the same Italian wine. Not that is wasn't good, it's just nice to have a change once in awhile," I said with a laugh.

"Here's to change!" she said as she poured us each a glass.

I raised my glass, "To change," I responded with all my heart.

"I'm so glad you're here, Leah. I've been worried about you. I thought he was too possessive."

"He's way too possessive," I agreed. "He's insanely jealous, and I mean insanely. I felt like I was suffocating. One day he's the nicest guy in the world and the next day he's the biggest asshole in the world. When I saw his hands on my kid, I got so angry, I mean who the hell does he think he is? I didn't even think about it, I just ran to my office and phoned the police." I paused for breath then added, "He's not stable, although he should be in a stable; the Italian stallion belongs in a stable," I said, unable to hold back my laughter. We both fell into a fit of giggles. It felt so good to be with my best friend.

Carrie kept trying to say something but she was laughing too hard to get the words out. We were practically hysterical. "Stallion — I think you mean jackass!" she was finally able to say after a deep breath. We relapsed back into gales of laughter. We laughed until tears rolled down our cheeks and our stomachs hurt. I was sure it was the best feeling in the world. Then her phone rang; we both jumped. "It's probably Ken," she said on her way over to the phone, "speaking of jackasses." Her comment drove us both into yet another fit of laughter. She was laughing so hard she couldn't answer the phone. It stopped ringing. We heard the answering machine pick it up.

"Hi, Carrie this is Joe."

We stopped laughing and looked at each other as we listened to the message. "It's nine-thirty right now; if it's not too late when you get in would you give me a call. It's very important. Thanks." He left a number then hung up. The sound of his voice made me feel sick to my stomach. I wondered if he'd ever be out of my life.

"That's his parent's phone number," I gasped. The stress of hearing his voice diminished a little as I realized he wasn't in my apartment. He wasn't close by. She asked where his parents lived. I told her they lived in the north end of the city, miles away. I got an idea. "I should go home and get all my business records while I know he's not there," I said, feeling a rush of excitement.

"I'll take you," she offered enthusiastically.

It felt eerie unlocking my door. I turned on the light then gasped in disbelief. My apartment was empty. I opened the door to the large storage room; it was empty, all my furniture and off-season clothes were gone. In the bedroom, my few sweaters and my family photo albums were on the floor. They had obviously been thrown there. The door to the office was closed, I pushed it open. It, too, was empty. My desk, photocopier, phone, fax machine, filing cabinet and all my files and business records were gone. "Jesus, Carrie, he stole my livelihood!" All hope I had of getting my business records disappeared. *I can't beat him.*

"What an asshole! He can't just take your stuff," Carrie said furiously. "Phone the police, Leah, don't let him get away with this. He's such a jerk!"

I had never seen Carrie look so angry or upset. I called the police. They informed me that because Joe and I were living together I would have to take him to civil court. "He stole all my business records and supplies. I work from home." I said fighting back tears. The officer suggested I talk to a lawyer.

I looked around the room. *This is just the beginning of his retaliation. He has to be stopped, but how?* I walked heavily into the kitchen and opened the cupboard doors. There were a couple of cups and a solitary plate. All my dishes, pots, pans and electrical appliances were gone. "I'm getting my stuff back!" I said to Carrie.

She looked baffled by the whole thing. She took hold of my hand. "Let's get out of here," she said, "it's giving me the creeps."

"He's nuts, I'm not kidding. He's such a fucking asshole; I'm sick of him taking everything from me," I said feeling a determination I hadn't felt for a long time.

She didn't ask me what I meant when I said I was sick of him taking everything from me. I told her I was going to phone him at his parents as soon as we got back to her place, adding that they didn't have call display, so he wouldn't know where I was calling from.

As soon as we got back to Carrie's house we noticed the blinking light on the answering machine. "It's probably just Ken," she said. The first message was from Ken. He said Joe had called him at work. "He's looking for Leah. I told him we hadn't heard a thing from her. Call me when you get in." The second message was from Joe.

"Sorry to bother you," he said, faking concern. "I'm really worried about Leah. I just want to make sure she's okay, please call me, Carrie. I know she'll contact you, you're her best friend. I have my pager from work." He left his pager number. He sounded frantic. I could see the rage on his face; his eyes narrow, his jaw tight. The fear these mental pictures produced must have shown on my face.

"What's really going on, Leah?" Carrie asked slowly. "There's a reason you're hiding from him." I looked down at my glass and nodded. I couldn't stand to tell her about the beatings, but I admitted I was afraid of him. I told her he had threatened to find and harm me if I ever left him.

"That's terrible Leah. He threatened you, stole from you and then he has the nerve to phone here pretending he's worried about you. I hate him." Her eyes flashed anger. "I figured you weren't happy. When you told me he gave you an engagement ring, you sounded depressed."

"I was confused about so many things. But I knew I didn't want to marry him," I said grimly. "Anyway, let's not talk about him. Let's just enjoy our evening."

Before long, we were laughing again. "We're like a couple of school girls," Carrie said.

"A couple of bad-ass school girls," I stated. We started singing the Cyndi Lauper song; *Girls Just Want to Have Fun.* I changed the lyrics and sang; *the phone rings in the middle of the night . . . and jackass Joe yells*

I'm ruining his life. Oh jackass Joe you're so stupid and dumb, girls just want to have fun.

We continued laughing and joking for the rest of the evening. Laughter truly is the best medicine and so is having a best friend like Carrie. Hanging out with her reminded me of the person I was before I met Joe. I slept soundly that night.

The next morning while having coffee with Carrie and Ken, Ken offered to go with me to find my furniture. "Where do think he has hidden it?" he asked. I told him it was probably in his parents' basement. I was reluctant to contact them in case Joe was there, but I had told Carrie I was going to call him, so I couldn't back down now.

I finished my coffee and phoned. Joe answered. My knees went weak and I took a quick breath. "Joe," I said, looking over at Carrie for reassurance. She smiled and looked at me as if to say, its okay, we're here. "I just left my apartment. Where the hell is all my stuff?' I asked firmly.

"Where are you? I've been worried about you. Are you okay?" he whined.

"I'm fine. I want my belongings back. I'm not talking to you again until you return it all." I was pleased my voice sounded strong.

"I didn't mean to take it. I told the movers what to take and they screwed up. It's all on its way to Vancouver. I'm moving back there. Honest, I swear on my life, Leah, they weren't supposed to take your things. I should have waited until they were finished but I left ahead of them. I went back later and saw what they did, but it was too late." He had hardly paused for breath during his unconvincing speech.

"I don't believe you. If my things aren't returned by suppertime, I'm calling the police." I could feel my spine strengthening. He let out a huff.

"Calm down, Leah. Meet me for lunch. Let's talk. I love you. I want to work things out. I want you to come to Vancouver with me, or we can stay here, whatever makes you happy. I'll go for counselling, that's a promise. I'll do anything to get you back. I love you so much."

I ignored his protestations and firmly told him I would call the police and press charges if he did not return my belongings. His reply told me more than he had intended.

"I'm not stupid, Leah. The police can't do anything about it, and I told you it was an accident. I'll get it back for you but it's going to take a while. I need to see you, this is bullshit. You're my fiancé and I don't know where you are. Is that fair?" I could feel his anger and it weakened me. I slammed the phone down.

"Didn't sound like that went very well," Ken said. "What can we do to help?"

I looked at his eyes; they were full of genuine concern and brotherly love. "Just what you're already doing; being the best friends in the world."

"Do you want me to kick his skinny ass?" he offered with a mischievous grin. I laughed, then unexpectedly burst into tears. They both jumped up and came to my side. I felt their arms around me and I thanked God for their love and friendship.

Once I calmed down, I told them what Joe said about the mover accidently taking my stuff. They both thought we should drive over to his parents' house and confront him. "It won't do any good. He's not going to let us in the house. He'd probably call the cops. I'm not kidding! Interesting how he knew I couldn't charge him with stealing my things. He obviously checked it out; he's probably done it before. All that furniture he has, I wouldn't be surprised to find he had stolen it from his ex-wife."

Just then the phone rang. Ken answered in a gruff voice. He was listening to Joe and looking at Carrie and me. He kept rolling his eyes and shaking his head in disgust. Finally he replied, "We don't know where she is. If she wanted us to know, she'd tell us, and if she wanted you to know she'd tell you. I don't want you phoning here anymore." He hung up, looked at me and said, "He sounds like he going off the deep end. Holy shit!"

"That's why I don't want him to know where I am. He'd never leave me alone. I shouldn't even have phoned him." My new-found confidence was ebbing. I knew he was going to keep on looking for me until he found me. I wondered if the only chance I had was to pretend I'd go back to him if he got help. It would buy me some time. I was sure he wouldn't kill me if he thought we were going to get back together. I voiced my thoughts. "Maybe I should be nice to him. If he thinks there's a chance of us getting back together, he might give me back my stuff."

"Won't that just drag it out? I mean, he has to accept the fact you left him. Sooner or later he has to accept that," Carrie said in a matter-of-fact tone.

"He's not the accepting type," I said, suppressing a cynical laugh at the understatement.

"Sooner or later he'll accept it. He has to, what else can he do?" Ken said encouragingly.

Kill me. He could kill me. I smiled in spite of my grim thoughts and nodded in agreement.

A while later Carrie drove me back to my aunt's. I was paranoid the whole time. I kept looking over my shoulder. I imagined him driving around and suddenly seeing me in Carrie's car. I imagined him following us.

"I'm worried about you, Leah. You're a nervous wreck," Carrie said as she pulled up to my aunt's house.

"I'm fine, Carrie. Don't worry," I said, trying to sound convincing. I hugged her then asked her not to pull away until I was inside. "Just in case my aunt isn't home. I don't have a key," I said to explain my request.

Shortly after, Chad phoned me. He said a detective had called him and wanted to talk to me. He said it had something to do with Joe. I felt my heart sink wondering what the hell Joe had involved me in. I asked Chad how the detective got his number and he explained he had given it to the police the day they came to my apartment. He gave me the detective's name, Detective Scott Stevens, and a number. I felt numb as I wrote down the information. I told Chad I would call him back after speaking with the detective.

I didn't want to phone in front of my aunt so I used the phone in the bedroom. I was nervous. The detective had a British accent. He said he was investigating charges that were laid against Joe in 1993. He said the charges were pressed by his ex-wife. He wanted me to meet with him and his partner. I hesitated at first. So many things were running through my head. *Why do they want to talk to me? If I tell them anything about Joe he'll kill me for sure. Besides, I can't prove anything.*

"I'm worried about your safety," the detective said. The words hit me in the gut. The detective obviously knew Joe was dangerous. I gave him Myla's address and said I would meet them there.

As soon as I hung up, I phoned Chad and told him about my scheduled meeting with the detectives. Then I phoned Carrie and told her about my conversation with Detective Stevens. She offered to come with me for moral support, but I told her I would be fine. I began to allow myself to believe the police would somehow protect me.

Chapter 21

I'D ALREADY BEEN at Myla's apartment for fifteen agonizing minutes when the detectives arrived. Detective Stevens introduced himself and his partner, Detective Bill Parker to me. They were both over six feet tall with broad shoulders and solid statures. They both looked kind and intelligent. I felt comfortable immediately.

Once we were sitting around the dining room table, Detective Stevens told me they had been asked by a prosecuting attorney named Selene Stephanopoulos to investigate Joe Pisano. He said Joe's ex wife, Julie, pressed charges against him two years ago when police were called to their residence. I soon learned that Julie had been staying at a women's shelter in Calgary when I met Joe. She had escaped from him only two months before. When she left the shelter she fled the country, in fact she fled the continent. I knew she had run away because she feared for her life.

"She's flown back here a few times to meet with Miss Stephanopoulos," Detective Parker said. "A couple of court dates were set but had to be postponed because Pisano didn't have legal counsel. He's fired seven lawyers."

"When the police came to my apartment they told me he didn't have a criminal record," I said, thinking they had made a mistake.

"He doesn't. He's been charged but not convicted — yet," Detective Stevens said. "We've been working on this case for quite some time and we're wondering if there's anything you'd like to tell us about him."

A rush of anxiety washed over me. I asked if they would mind if I had a cigarette. Detective Stevens lit my cigarette then his own. "I have plenty to tell but I'm scared. I'm scared of him and what he'll do if he finds out I talked to the police about him. He'll go crazy, or should I say crazier?" I could feel my body trembling and hear it in my voice.

"Although I can't guarantee anything, I'm pretty sure he's going to serve time. I can't tell you anything about the case except that the charges are serious," Detective Stevens said seriously.

Hearing the detective say Joe was probably going to jail sounded like the best chance I had of being free and safe.

"He stole my furniture, all my business and personal item," I blurted out, then quickly explained what I did for a living. "He said he took it by accident and it's en route to Vancouver. I think it's probably in his parents' basement."

They both looked at me with empathy. I started talking, spilling out bits and pieces of my experience with him. I told them about the horrific abuse. The more I revealed, the calmer I became. At one point I agreed to give them a statement.

It took three days to complete my forty-two page statement and another three days to process it. It was difficult to tell them things I swore I would never tell anyone. So many times throughout the process of giving my statement I felt I was confessing to being a complete fool. Not that they ever made me feel that way; just the opposite in fact. They combated my humiliation by treating me with the utmost respect.

"I know this isn't easy; I admire your courage, Leah," Detective Stevens said to me several times.

I was amazed at how the detectives put the evidence together. They talked to Chad, Carrie and Ken about my change in personality and the phone calls Joe was continuing to make to them. We went to my apartment and they took pictures of the damage he'd done; fist holes in two doors, the broken closet door and blood stains from my nose bleed on the carpet. They said they'd talk to Myla when she returned from her trip. As soon as my statement was processed, they read me the list of charges; assault, aggravated assault, assault with a weapon (scissors), unlawful confinement, destruction of property (burning my clothes), intercepting private communication and theft over one thousand dollars. I was stunned. I hadn't realized how criminal his activities really were or that I could charge him.

During the six days I had been working with the detectives, Joe was still making frantic phone calls to Carrie at home and Ken at work. He was calling my son at work and begging him to pass on messages to me. I was almost out of my mind with worry. The detectives told me that once he was arrested, he would be held in custody for thirty days for a psychiatric evaluation. I was looking forward to thirty days of peace, but I was terrified he'd find me before he was arrested. I tried not to think about what might happen after the thirty days. I could only cross one bridge at a time.

Joe was arrested. Detective Stevens phoned me as soon as he had been taken into custody. I started to breathe again. I phoned Chad right away, then I called Carrie. I still hadn't told her and Ken about the abuse.

That evening I went over to Carrie's house. Ken was at work. I told her what the charges were all about. She listened quietly while I talked. I had a difficult time looking her in the eyes for fear of seeing her disappointment in me. I felt disgraced and soiled. She asked me why I didn't tell her. She said I could have come to her and Ken any time. I understood her response yet I felt judged. I wondered if I would ever regain my self-respect. I wondered if I would ever feel clean again. I squirmed in my chair. Sensing my discomfort, she reached over and gently squeezed my hand. Her touch was consoling; I relaxed a little.

"Carrie, I don't know how to explain what it was like without sounding ridiculous. It's embarrassing. I never thought I'd be in a situation like that. I mean, I didn't think it could happen to me. Maybe someday, after I have some distance from it all and do some healing, I'll be able to explain it better. I don't even understand the hold he had on me. I do know my fear was real, but I saw it as my problem I didn't feel I had the right to put anyone else in danger. I was overwhelmed, Carrie. I don't know what would have happened if Chad hadn't come over that day. He has no idea what he actually saved me from. He's my hero. Both of them are. Chad and Myla knew something was wrong and wanted to check on me. Honestly Carrie, if I hadn't left I think he would have killed me eventually."

Carrie was a rock. She bolstered my spirits by telling me she was proud of me for leaving, that it took courage, and she assured me I already looked stronger, more like my old self. When I told her I felt bad about Joe harassing her, she replied in typical Carrie fashion.

"You shouldn't feel bad. He's the lunatic. I couldn't believe some of the things he said to me. For instance, he told me you faked orgasms!" She started chuckling, "I said to him, you mean like in *When Harry Meets Sally*. We both laughed heartily.

"I did!" I said after we stopped laughing. "Sometimes I felt like the sex was the only normal thing about our relationship, it's what couples do. Or at least that's what I told myself, but the truth is it was awful. It's so degrading to share a bed with the same guy who beats the crap out of you. I didn't dare say no to him, but I sure in hell wasn't going to have an orgasm, at least I could control that. My God Carrie, I was sleeping with a psychopath!" I looked at my friend and saw her willingness to try to understand. "You know those dreams where you try to scream for help but nothing will come out, or you try to run from danger but your legs won't move?" Carrie nodded and said she'd had those dreams many times. "That's what it was like with him; a nightmare, except I was awake."

"I feel guilty that I didn't pry when I felt something was wrong," she said with tears in her eyes. "I had a bad feeling but then I thought, Leah is so strong and independent, she can take care of herself, she won't put up with any crap. I never suspected you were being abused, I just thought he was very needy and possessive."

I begged her not to feel guilty for not picking up on what I had hidden so well, then we started talking about when I first met Joe.

"I understand how you fell for him. I remember when you first started going out with him I was kind of envious of all the romantic things he did. I used to think; I wish Ken would buy me roses, nice gifts for no reason and take me out for romantic dinners. I thought you were lucky having a great looking, charming guy who adored you and wanted to spoil you," she said shaking her head.

"My mom used to say, be careful what you wish for — you might get it!" I said smiling at the wisdom of those words.

"Hey, I've always been curious about the undershirt. Did he ever take it off?" She had a mischievous grin on her face. "Stella!" she yelled, making us both laugh.

"He owned seven of them, one for each day of the week and all exactly the same. He didn't have a tattoo or birthmark, although I did check to see if he was hiding three sixes," I joked. "He just liked wearing an undershirt, even in hot weather and even to bed. The only time he wasn't wearing one was when he showered. I asked once what was with the undershirt, he said he didn't like being completely naked. Isn't it kind of symbolic though, Carrie? I mean, I thought he was trying to hide something and subconsciously he was —his true colours."

We looked at each other as though we had uncovered one of the greatest mysteries in the world, and we agreed a woman's intuition is a powerful tool — if you listen to it.

The next day Detective Stevens called to tell me my belongings were indeed in the Pisano's basement. He asked me to meet him there to identify everything. Another woman was there when I arrived; Lisa, the mother of Joe's child. She was very attractive, graceful and soft spoken. I learned she and her daughter had moved back to Calgary more than a year ago. Joe knew nothing about it. His parental rights had been taken away years ago. She had never lived in New York; she lived in Vancouver. Her friends told Joe she was in New York to protect her. I thought about the phone conversations he claimed he had with his daughter. Once a week or so he'd tell me he had stopped in at his parents' house on his way home from work and phoned her. He said he called her from there so they could talk to her too. He often bragged about the generous child support he paid. I shuddered at the lengths he had gone to in order to deceive me, but I wasn't shocked.

All the furniture Joe was so proud of belonged to Lisa. She had also escaped to a women's shelter and while she was there, he stole her furniture.

After I pressed charges, Lisa decided to press charges too. She said after learning about Julie and me she didn't feel so alone. The case against him was getting stronger and stronger.

Once I had my belongings, I moved back into my apartment. Rather than letting the bad memories make me feel uncomfortable, I revelled in the feeling that I had reclaimed what was mine. I didn't care at that point if it was just for thirty days; I was going to enjoy the peace. I planned that if he was released after his thirty day evaluation, I would go back to my aunt until I found another place to live. Now that the police had investigated him, I wasn't sure whether he would be afraid to harass or harm me or my loved ones, or whether he would be bent on revenge. I knew it must be driving him crazy that I was free and he was locked up. I also knew he'd blame me for that. I became more and more anxious as the thirty days drew to an end.

He wasn't released. His psychiatric evaluation was kept confidential until after the trial so I didn't know the details, but I was extremely grateful the justice system recognized he was dangerous. He remained in custody for another fourteen months awaiting his trial.

I met Julie at the court house. It was an emotional meeting. She was beautiful and delicate. I saw her innocence immediately; a light came on inside me, showing me my own innocence. The heavy cloak of shame I still wore felt a little lighter.

The trial lasted two weeks. We all testified against him. The day of the sentencing, Julie, Lisa and I sat side by side in the front row of the courtroom. We held hands tightly as the judge read the sentence. Between the three of us twenty charges had been laid. He was found guilty of nineteen and sentenced to ten years in prison. Ten years sounded like a lifetime of freedom to each of us. We hugged and cried tears of joy. Justice was served.

That evening Julie, Lisa and I celebrated with Chad, Myla, Carrie, Ken, Detective Stevens, Detective Parker, and Selene Stephanopoulos. We celebrated for the women who would be safe from him for the next ten years. We celebrated hope, freedom and new beginnings.

Epilogue

HEALING FROM MY experience has been a long and often difficult journey. Victims of domestic violence are often judged by society harsher than the perpetrators. The court case received a lot of local news coverage and so friends, acquaintances and colleagues knew more than I would have told them. Some were supportive and understanding, some weren't. I was told more than once by other women they would never have put with it. I was given all kinds of advice on what I should have done. I was asked why I didn't leave. *I did leave.* This sort of advice and questioning fed my shame, but eventually I learned not to worry about what others thought. I knew I probably thought the same way before it happened to me.

Carrie never judged me. She stood by me every step of the way. The court case went on for two weeks, she showed up every day to be there for me. My business had started falling apart during the last couple of months I was with Joe. She came and worked with me, she became my business partner, and together we built the business back up.

A few years ago I started speaking publicly about relationship violence to high school students. I told them what warning signs to look for, and what irrational behaviour could lead to. I was nervous the first few times I did my presentations so Carrie came with me and sat proudly in the front row. When I told her I was writing a book, she encouraged me.

When I told her I didn't think I could write it, she convinced me I could. I wish everyone had a friend like Carrie.

Lisa and I meet for lunch once in awhile. She's happy and healthy. Her husband is a great person and her daughter, Alexandra, recently graduated from law school. Julie lives a wonderful life in Hawaii with her husband. She tells me it's like living in paradise.

As for me, about a year after the court case I went on a date with Terry. We've been together ever since. He's a wonderful husband and friend. I'm peaceful and happy.

Joe applied for parole three times during his incarceration and each time he was denied. He served his full sentence and was released under strict conditions and monitoring. He never took responsibility, and he has never shown signs of remorse for his actions or empathy for his victims. His psychological assessment revealed he had a list of mental conditions I had never heard of. In plain English, he was a psychopath. The last I heard about him through the monitoring system was that he is living in northern Alberta.

I'm grateful to the detectives who worked hard on this case and for the compassion, support and respect they showed Julie, Lisa and me. I'm grateful to the crown prosecutor for fighting to reclaim the stolen dignity of three women. But I'm most grateful for the unconditional love and support from the people I admire most in this world; my children.